ITHACA

SUSAN FISH

SUSAN FISH

ISBN 978-0-9938903-0-7
Published by Storywell
October 1, 2014

Cover image used with permission of Ithaca
and Tompkins County Tourism.

Always keep Ithaca fixed in your mind
to arrive there is your ultimate goal
but do not hurry the voyage at all.
It is better to let it last for long years
and even to anchor at the isle when you are old
rich with all you have gained on the way
-Ithaka by Constantine Cadavy

To my grandma—Dorothy Mae Besterd Cowin—
with whom Daisy and I shared a love of cooking for a crowd,
and so much more

Contents

ITHACA

August 2009
Ithaca, New York

1
Tomato-Basil Bisque

Help out. Those were the magic words that had colored my whole existence. You could always count on Daisy to help out. Some people might have paid attention to the words, would you like to, but it was the last few words that made me say yes. And Henry was right. I did like honey.

He had phoned on a Friday morning in late August. "Look, I know how much you like honey and I was wondering. Today is the perfect weather to harvest it and I was wondering whether you'd like to come with me to help out."

"Sure."

"It'll take most of the day," he said. "But I could drive you back after lunch if you have plans."

Dear God, my plans for the day included Oprah mostly, and planning next week's soup. Although with an abundance of tomatoes and zucchini everywhere, I had a good idea already what next Wednesday's soup would be. Which left me with Oprah on a hot late August afternoon. I thought maybe she could do without me for the day.

"What should I bring?" I asked.

"Wear long sleeves and pants. White if you've got them. And a hat. I've got water at the cabin. And we can pick up some hamburgers when we need a break. Would you be ready in an hour?"

I'd always been an early riser, which made my days even longer these days, so other than changing my clothes, I was more than ready now.

"Sure," I said, reaching into the fridge for the half-dozen eggs I had boiled last night, egg salad sandwiches being one thing I didn't mind eating alone. I would make deviled eggs to bring along.

It had been a long time since a man had asked me out, and this, I was fairly certain, was not a date. Henry's wife had multiple sclerosis. I gathered Jane was largely confined to her bed although she could move around by wheelchair. Henry had taken early retirement to look after her.

Jane had worked at Cornell as a secretary, and for a while she had worked in the geology department where Arthur was. It was then that she and Henry had started coming out to the Wednesday suppers. After Henry started his beekeeping, he had begun bringing honey, small bottles of it, to Wednesday night suppers.

By the time Henry showed up an hour later, the deviled eggs had become part of a full picnic lunch. As I climbed into his minivan, I realized it was the first time I could remember being in the passenger seat since Arthur's funeral. It felt like such a kindness not to have to drive, not to have to watch where I was going. For the first time all summer, I could look outside and see the tall grasses on either side of the car, the tangle of wildflowers, the dust of insects flying above them. It made me think of our task.

"So," I said, smoothing my slacks, "tell me what we do."

Henry looked over at me and I was reminded what a distinguished-looking man he was. Most of us faded or sagged as we got older, but occasionally there was a man like Henry.

"You mean the honey?" he asked.

"Yes."

"Well," he said, "first of all, we hope that the bees are all taking advantage of the beautiful weather to go out and gather nectar, so we can take racks of honey. And then, we smoke out any bees that are left inside. And then, we carry the racks to the car."

Henry had a small sliver of property on a small lake about fifteen minutes away from Ithaca. As we drove, he told me about the process of making honey, and how he had gotten into beekeeping in the first place. I knew it had to do with Jane but I wasn't sure how.

"When we found out she had MS," he said, "we read everything we possibly could and we heard lots about royal jelly being a great healer for myelin sheath damage." He reminded me of Arthur, who taught me geological terms simply by using them in context. Oprah always explained things. I could feel my brain opening up for the first time in months. I stretched my legs and asked more questions.

That was how it worked: a catechistic conversation, where I asked questions and Henry answered. We passed a succession of homemade signs that said No Fracking, and I idly wondered what they meant, but I was trying to pay attention to what Henry was saying. By the time we reached the property, I knew a number of new terms and facts, about bees and honey and multiple sclerosis.

Henry's beekeeping vocabulary, like Arthur's geological terms, was a matter of choice, words lapped up in a quest for knowledge and understanding. How different the words that came with illness, words that labeled worries, that gave amateurs a professional vocabulary in a field in which they were victims, or worse, helpless bystanders. My vocabulary was cardiology, Henry's was multiple sclerosis, and my friend Cecily's was oncology. Even to label it thus—rather than heart or cancer—showed that we had negotiated the system and learned enough of the local language to be able to barter and beg.

Henry turned off onto a rutted laneway and raised dust as he went. We had driven with the windows up and the air conditioning on—I hadn't wanted to ask whether he minded if I opened the window as I always did when Arthur and I drove—so it was only after he turned the car off and I opened my door that the smells and the sounds hit my ear. And the heat. I had forgotten that it was a day that promised intense heat and when I opened the car door, the whine of the cicadas hit my ear along with the smells of new-mown hay and fresh lake water. I left my picnic basket inside the van but I brought my water bottle and my hat out with me. Henry moved to the back of the van and began carrying out equipment. I stood by, nurse to his doctor, ready to help if he needed it. I looked about me and saw no evidence of hives but I could see bees in the morning sunlight, and a small cabin lower on the property, near the water that was sparkling below us.

"It was a fishing camp," Henry said, as he reached for the last of the equipment. "They divided it up fifteen years ago, and I bought my section eight years ago."

I nodded.

"Here," he said, and handed me a veil. I put my hat on and my veil on top. A veil. Arthur had died seven months before our fortieth wedding anniversary. Ruby. That was how grief went—unexpected private wells and weeks of emptiness. But Henry was handing me equipment so I blinked and tried to focus.

"Can you manage this?" he asked and it was small and lightweight.

"Of course," I said. I could always manage.

"Of course you can," he said, and a pained look crossed his face. I knew he was thinking of Jane and I didn't know how to feel.

"So where are the hives?" I asked, to distract him.

"Up the hill," he said. "Do you see the path?" He pointed at a well-trodden lane. "I run out here sometimes," he said. "It's what keeps me sane. People say you tell your secrets to the bees but I like to come and listen to them. I run out here and fall asleep, listening to the hum of the hive. And then I can face it again."

It. He made me realize there were different kinds of grief, different ways to lose someone you loved. It could be utterly unexpected as it was for Arthur or slow and excruciating as it was for Jane and Henry. There was sometimes a competition between caregivers of sick people—I had seen that after Arthur's first heart attack—but there was a surprising absence of rivalry between those who grieved, and a lack of curiosity too. It was as if bearing our own burdens was more than enough—there was no space for prurient interest or one-upmanship. There was also one slight surprise: what I had to remind myself each time I heard someone else's story was that they did not have to bear what I did in addition to what they carried—each of us had our own burdens and managed them as best we could. I wondered whether the hum of bees would be good for me too.

He collected a handful of pine needles from the ground under a stand of trees and squashed them into a small canister, releasing the unexpected scent of Christmas.

"It's a smoker," he said, pulling out a lighter. "It calms the bees."

He looked otherworldly in his gear, gently spraying puffs of smoke into the hives, and I stood back and watched. He was stung twice—and he sent me for meat tenderizer and water from the cabin after the first sting—but he considered it both a small price to pay and a relatively unscathed harvest. The first year, he said, he had had thirty-seven stings—Jane had counted them and treated them. He had not known about meat tenderizer, but she had known and had driven out to get some from town. That was when she was still driving, was still able to come out to the cabin.

The cabin itself was thin-walled, with sunlight seeping through the spaces between the boards. There was a kitchen sink and a toilet, and a single camp bed with two army blankets and no pillow. There was a shelf where honey tins and glass jars sat next to several warped books. There were two mousetraps. I found the jar of meat tenderizer and I refilled my water bottle at the sink. The smell of lake water came out of the tap and I let it run a minute to try to get colder water, but it stayed the same temperature so I filled my bottle and shut the door behind me.

Henry stopped when he saw me coming.

"You mix it in your hand like a paste," he said. He rolled up his shirtsleeve where a bee had gotten between his gloves and his shirt. His arm was hairy and muscular. I wondered if he meant for me to make the paste but I handed him the jar and the water bottle.

When he was properly anointed, we carried frames of honey, set in tubs, down to his van.

"Don't you love the smell?" Henry said as we opened the door with the final, third frame. I breathed in greedily.

"Sunshine and rain, clover and wildflowers," I said and then I felt silly, like I had recited a poem.

"You have a good sniffer," Henry said, closing the trunk and reaching in his pocket for his keys. "So can I take you out for a hamburger?"

"I made lunch," I said. "I made a picnic lunch."

He looked at me then with eyes of wonder.

"It's in the front," I said and I found the insulated oilskin bag, red plaid, from where I had put it at my feet.

"I thought that was your purse," Henry said, taking the lunch bag. "Come on—let's sit down by the water. The bees'll be riled up for a while. I'd rather give them their space."

I followed him down the path. My sniffer could smell him then too, the one element that wasn't late summer meadow, a smell of clean sweat and musk, a morning's hard work. We walked past the cabin and I saw a low, dilapidated wooden dock, hovering just above the water, in the shadow of a willow tree. I must have hesitated because Henry turned.

"Oh," he said. "Did you want to freshen up?"

"I just need to wash my hands," I said.

"Well, you can do that up there or down here. It's the same water."

"But you have soap up there?" I said.

"Dish soap," he replied.

"That's fine."

Someone once said that we all had a limit of words each day. I felt like I had been storing mine up and today was a day to spend them—and yet, I'd become used to economizing.

Henry waited outside while I washed my hands. I washed the back of my neck too and felt cooler. I wished for a mirror to know whether I needed to brush my hair or not, remembered that my brush was at home, and I ran damp fingers through it, patting it and shaping it as I would bread dough, into what I hoped was some degree of order. Then I washed my hands again and stepped outside.

Henry was watching something. He raised a hand without

looking back at me. "Look, Jane," he said. "A hummingbird."

And there it was, a shimmer of grace, green and red.

It was not until Henry went inside and I heard him relieving himself—which was such an intimate, normal sound that I walked down toward the dock to offer him some privacy—that I heard his words again. I had heard the "Look" and I had looked, but he had called me Jane. He could not have known. He was thinking of Jane who was at home in her wheelchair. My head started to throb and I wasn't sure it was the heat. He could not have known what the J in Mrs. J. Daisy Turner stood for. No one had called me Jane in more than fifty years.

The cabin door banged shut above me and Henry had rolled up his sleeves and pant legs. "Look," he said again as he caught up to me. "I've got root beer to contribute." He picked up my lunch bag and stepped carefully onto the dock and turned to reach out a hand to help me aboard. Everything in me saw the scene in judgment, and the wood bobbed and swayed under our feet.

He squeezed my hand. "Don't worry. It'll hold. Well, it'll hold one of us at least." I froze. "And it's all of a foot of water. Two feet at the end." I relaxed and let go but then I stepped on a rotting board and Henry was at my elbow. "I usually sit here," he said. "Put my feet in the water and call myself lucky. Do you want a chair?"

"Would this dock hold two people and a chair?" I asked.

"Good point. Well, I'll help you up again afterwards."

Would he help with getting moss stains off my white slacks,

I wondered, but I sat and watched as he peeled off his shoes and socks and sank his feet into the water.

I opened the picnic bag and I felt like a conjuror—a jar of pickles, the deviled eggs (still freezing cold in the ice pack), half a loaf of pumpernickel bread left from Wednesday night, and some hummus. I had wrapped peaches in paper towels to keep them from bruising.

Henry unwrapped his peach and set the paper towel on his lap. My legs felt awkward—it had been a long time since I had sat cross-legged. I tried sitting side-saddle but we almost lost the root beer then.

"You'll have to join me," Henry said, waving long brown feet through the water. I turned away to take my shoes off and my socks, and I stacked them behind me, a little something to lean against. I felt shy about Henry watching my feet so I pointed out across the lake and asked about a bird I could see as I slid my feet into water my son Nick used to call room temperature water. Nick liked his water icy cold, so cold it would hurt my teeth. This water was fresh as springtime and without thinking, I sighed with pleasure.

"See," he said, handing me back my bottle of root beer. "I told you."

We broke off chunks of bread and dipped it in the hummus. Henry finished the pickles and poured the brine into the lake—"salt water"—and fished out the garlic and the dill and chewed them both.

My peach was perfectly ripe and dripped on the paper towel in my lap and I licked my fingers clean.

"That," he said, leaning back, "that was a feast. Thank you."

"Can I ask you something?" I said, watching my feet appear and disappear in the dark water. "Why did you ask me today?"

"To come here?" he said. "I needed an extra pair of hands and I thought you could use something different."

I drew my legs out of the water, suddenly chilled, and wrapped my arms around my knees. My back would ache tonight.

"How are you doing, Daisy?" he asked.

It was the question that could dissolve me, the question I dreaded. I watched a dragonfly over the water and I decided he had no right to ask.

"Did you know that people believed that after someone died, if the deceased had been a good man, a daisy flower would begin to grow on its own?" I had heard people do this on NPR, ignore a question, take the conversation to the ground they wanted. I didn't want to cry.

He looked at me then, distracted from his question, and I looked away. "I know that bees collect pollen from daisies," he said.

"So, what happens now, to your honey?" I asked, tired already of flower trivia.

"Now, I take it home to my garage. I use an extractor to spin the comb and extract the honey and then I bottle it up. Want to watch?"

"Thanks, but there are things I have to do, things I planned to do today."

"And I've kept you out. I'm sorry."

"No, no. I've enjoyed today." I started to feel blood rise in my cheeks and then I remembered that Henry had asked me out of pity and at least there was nothing to apologize for. But neither did I want to face Henry's Jane.

"We'd better go then," he said, and he pulled me to my feet.

"Thank you," I said and I slid my feet into my shoes. I gathered up what I had brought and Henry collected the bottles.

The smell of the honey was almost overpowering when we reached the van.

"Like it?" Henry asked, inhaling.

I could only nod. Daisies come up faithfully each year in the garden, even if children pick them. They are cheerful in drought, constant in rain and wind.

"What are these signs?" I asked when we had passed our third or fourth "NO FRACKING" sign.

"It's that oil drilling thing," Henry said. "They found pockets of oil and gas in the shale here and they think they can get it out."

"But people think it's a bad idea?" I said.

"There've been letters to the editor about it in the paper."

All I had read of the paper in the last four months was the obituaries—largely keeping track of who had joined the widow club and at what age people died. I had stopped circling sales, even.

"What's the problem?" I asked. It was a question, really, for Arthur, not Henry, I realized with a sting.

We were turning onto my street. "I'm not sure," he
said. "Some people think it can wreck the water or cause
earthquakes." He pulled into my driveway. "Do you want a
chunk of comb?" he asked. "Or should I just bring you some
of our honey later?"

"Thank you," I said, as he handed me a small piece of
honeycomb that dripped on my hands. "I had a nice time."

Something had shifted in me, something deep. I had
forgotten I was alive until that day. It might have been the
simple pleasures of a picnic and a conversation, of a man
who smelled good and honey that carried the scent of every
wildflower in the area. It might have been sunshine and lake
water. It might have been helping and sitting in the passenger
seat, having a man carry my bag again, having my hands
drenched in honey. It might even have been a coincidence.
Henry had said earthquake and as I walked toward my house,
I felt a small tremor, something that reminded me I was still
alive.

I walked around to the back of my house where I knew I had
a stack of yogurt containers. Carefully, I put the honey in
one, and licked my hands clean. Then I turned on the garden
hose and washed them in icy water, wiping my hands on my
already-filthy pants.

I took my shoes and socks off when I got into the house
and I didn't even look through the mail. I put the small

stack of envelopes on the table and the container of honey. I walked through my house barefoot, which was something I almost never did. My feet felt new-baptized, sensitive, and I felt the thick shag of the gold carpet Arthur had put in when we first moved there, the carpet Nick laughed at. I felt the coolness of the linoleum in the kitchen, the patio stones in the backyard. I sat in the backyard for a while, watching insects at work, unsure what to do next.

Henry had told me about the bees and how they worked. I confessed that I had only ever seen the bees as individuals, and predators really—out to sting you if you weren't careful—with honey as a by-product. He had told me about the queen, the drones, the workers. How a bee might make a teaspoonful of honey in her lifetime—which was only six weeks. How bees fanned the nectar until it made honey. How bees would never eat the honey they had made themselves— they stored it away for those to come and ate that which had been left to them.

And what had been left to me? This house. And Wednesday nights. And Arthur's papers.

That was what was next, I realized. It was time to open the door to his study. When Arthur died, I had closed the door to his study, as I often did when he was traveling, simply so that I would not have to face the chaos of his papers. I had helped him type his papers, but the study had been his world, not mine. I had quickly gotten rid of Arthur's clothes, had thrown them away in black garbage bags, and I hadn't regretted my haste, but it had been easiest to keep the door to the study closed.

I wondered if we had any more soft drinks. I could use some sugar to bolster me. I went inside and down into the cool basement where we had a small old refrigerator humming away. Arthur and Nick had stocked it with soda for when they watched television. Occasionally I used it if there was no room for soups upstairs. But I hadn't stocked much food the last few years. I really should unplug the fridge in the basement, I thought. It must be costing a fortune in electricity. There was no root beer in the fridge, but there was a pair of Cokes. I didn't think soft drinks went bad, so I took one and carried it upstairs, unopened, to Arthur's study.

I stood outside Arthur's study a minute before I took a deep breath and opened the door. The room smelled stale and it smelled like Arthur.

I opened the window and leaned against the sill. I could hear a lawnmower up the street and the light coming in was dappled green and gold, and I needed the present to hold me very close because the past was threatening to engulf me. There were notes on the desk where he had laid aside his pen. There was a suit jacket on the coat-tree. There were the printouts I had typed for him the day before he died.

What survives us, I thought. The wind could pick up the papers in a moment. I could set fire to every one of them and they'd be gone. And yet, they remained and my husband was gone.

I sat down at the desk, feeling as I always did that I was invading Arthur's privacy, his sanctum. I thought of the bees and how Henry had subdued them into letting him take trays of their honey, with smoke. Henry had said that tending bees took courage and stillness. How could I do likewise, I wondered?

Arthur had never taken food or drink into his study, I remembered as I sat there with my can of Coke. I put it on the nape of my neck, and it was blessedly cool, and then on my forehead. I was going to take the can downstairs because I was thirsty, and suddenly it came to me that this was my study now, that these were my papers, my books, my room, my choices, my life.

There were reasons not to eat or drink in the study, though, or at least not at the desk. I went back to the window sill and opened my Coke and drank it down. And then I wondered how to start. I remembered being a teenager, having to clean out my granddaddy's garage and having literally no idea where to start, paralyzed by the enormousness of the task ahead of me.

I still felt sticky with honey and dirt. I left the door open and I went and washed up properly.

And then I circled the room again, damp and still uncertain. I sat back at the desk and adjusted the seat so that it was comfortable for me. I stood up again and took Arthur's coat out into the hall where I wouldn't be distracted by it. I looked at the paper on top of the rest and saw again the word I had seen on the signs.

"OK, Arthur," I said, probably aloud. "So what's fracking?"

It was when it became hard to read that I looked up and

realized it was evening, that I had missed Oprah, supper and most of the day. I was hungry and I had to pee desperately. But I knew what fracking was and why so many people were concerned about drilling through shale.

I went downstairs as if I was waking up. The heat had broken and my feet were cold now; I found slippers. I looked in the refrigerator and the cupboards and I didn't want any of the choices. I thought of what Henry had said about a hamburger earlier in the day, and I decided to walk downtown to get a burger. I put on a sweatercoat and locked the door behind me.

The sky was violet, the beautiful time of day. I had always liked that time, when the day's work was done and peace descended, and yet I didn't remember when I had last walked after sunset. It wasn't dark yet and I felt safe. I exchanged greetings—"beautiful evening" "yes it is" "nice night" "hello there Daisy"—with several neighbors sitting on their porches and I wondered whether they wondered at me.

The streets in late August were filled with impossibly young faces, away from home for the first time, dazzled by new tastes, sights and smells, whether a visible thong or a Thai restaurant.

I found myself in a fluorescent-lit restaurant, dazzled by the choices. Good cooks rarely go to restaurants. The teenager behind the counter asked what I wanted on my burger and it was mine to choose. "For here or to go?" he asked. I was not ready to sit alone in a molded-plastic seat. "To go, thanks."

I carried my little paper bag down to the lake, the big lake.

It was full dusk now, and I wondered if it was safe, but I had the cell phone Nick had bought me in my pocket and that seemed safe enough.

I found a glider swing by the water and watched the ducks settling for the night and some still out on the water. People rollerbladed past—another sign the students were back in town—and nodded to me. I opened my hamburger and took it out with an appetite. I could see the market building, dark, not far away. Within a few hours, vendors would be setting up for the market the next morning. I hadn't thought about the menu for Wednesday night yet, I realized with a start. But then I remembered a recipe I hadn't made it years, a tomato-basil bisque. It called for sugar to soften the acidity, but I thought maybe I could use honey instead. Yes, I could.

I looked out across the water. It had been a long day but time had not weighed on me for more than a few moments. And my hamburger was delicious.

2
Lentil-Carrot Soup
with Lime and Cumin

I should explain about Wednesday nights. It started when Arthur was new at the university, new and assigned grad students. It had been my idea for him to get to know his students outside of school, off campus. I had suggested they come over for supper. And so they did and so they devoured the food I made them. And no one suspected how young I was. We invited them back and soon it became a standing date in our calendar. They brought their girlfriends and then their wives. Sometimes Arthur's colleagues would come too. When Nick was a toddler, he loved having the students over, loved the energy of the house.

Eventually it drifted away from any affiliation with the school and it just became Wednesday night. I made pots and pots of soup, a different kind each week. I stocked up on bowls and spoons at garage sales and estate sales, mismatched bowls. You might get a bone china bowl or a wobbly earthenware bowl made in someone's pottery craze.

What I liked most about Wednesday nights was that it unstratified life. Not like drilling through shale would, but more like a beach where pebbles of granite rolled against shards of shale and every other kind of rock. I had once seen a photograph of sand magnified and it was a collection of exquisite jewels, every grain distinct and carried from afar. I liked rock beaches, though, where I could find small eggs to carry home in my pocket, run my thumb over. Every one of my coats had a stone or two in the pockets—not like that writer who filled her pockets and waded into the water—but still the stones grounded me. I could remember where some of them came from—a beach in England we visited when Arthur was at a conference, a small slide of a rock from Singapore when we visited Nick that one time and where the beach was a relief from the sparseness of the city.

Wednesday nights were like that too. At first, it had all been Arthur's students but even then there had been diversity, men and women, kids with different accents. Now the accents came from around the world and there were people of all ages there. So much of life was divided by age groups, even at church, where I was now expected to be part of the seniors group. Something in me was drawn to the young energy of people. I liked too watching people meet who would never meet otherwise, even in a small city the size of ours. Here they scooped soup for one another, asked questions of each other. I had seen friendships develop and even one marriage come out of Wednesday nights. I liked seeing professors holding babies of grad students, watching the wives who barely spoke English hold their hands over their mouths and giggle.

The Wednesday after Arthur died was the only time I lost track of time. People showed up at my house all the same, death or no death, and when there was no food made, they took to the kitchen themselves and made me food, spooned me back into the land of the living. That was a lentil-carrot soup with lime and cumin. I remember that one, flavorful after a week of tunafish sandwiches and cream cheese pinwheels.

After that, I kept up with the bare bones of my life, the obligations, so that no one knew how utterly empty my house was, my days were. They saw me on Wednesday evenings for the Wednesday suppers and then the house was filled with interesting people and good smells, laughter and conversation. The Wednesday suppers were a sort of lifeline for me. They didn't know that I left the dishes until the next day so that I would have something to do on Thursdays, that I planned the following week's supper on Friday, went to the market on Saturday, to church and to teach Sunday School on Sunday, and usually made the soup on Tuesday— because most soups would improve with sitting for a day. It was Mondays that I had to get through, Mondays that had no task whatsoever. Mondays are typically gray days for anyone but for someone with an utterly empty life, they are very hard. Mondays were the days I stayed in my housecoat and watched hours of television shows, just to hear a human voice.

I heard the word again on Wednesday night. Fracking.

You hear a new word and then you see it everywhere. That's always been my experience anyhow. I remember when I first heard the word yuppies, when they were building that new subdivision on Eastlake. I misheard the person talking about it and I thought they said puppies, and even though the word was everywhere after that, it always made me smile, thinking of how doglike the yuppies were, following their noses, eager to have their bellies scratched and to chase after every new bone.

And now it was fracking. I wondered if I had heard the word before. I didn't remember Arthur using it, and it wasn't in anything I had typed for him, but it was there on his desk, new articles and abstracts. If I had heard the term on a Wednesday night before, I would have heard it as a swear word, a politer version of the F word, probably. I remember when Nick was a little boy, he used to come home for lunch and he'd watch the Flintstones while he ate—I'm quite certain fracking was one of Fred Flintstone's swear words.

And then I heard it again.

My house was quiet until about quarter to six and then the door began its regular open and shut rhythm, and they began to come in, always mid-conversation, so that I let the words roll over me like waves of sound, and I smiled and did the things I could have done days before—folding cloth napkins, setting out glasses and stacks of bowls—and the things I could only do at the last minute—stirring the bisque and adding ladles. The house filled with chatter and laughter, and I gave the illusion that my life, too, was filled with activity. I heard someone say Lee Henshall—"no, she sold her house and moved last year"—and football—"Saturday at two"—and then I saw Cecily and she carried loaves of bread from the restaurant like she was Miss America and they were her flowers. I followed her into the kitchen and she began to cut the bread while I shook a tea towel into a basket and began to fill it with the slices of bread. People started to line up for soup, and I was drawn into conversation. And then Henry was before me, carrying a jar of honey, the color of amber. He opened it up and held it out to me to smell and it felt like the priest offering me communion and my eyes closed as I breathed it in.

"Sunshine and rain and flowers?" he asked over the sounds of talk and clattering spoons, and I knew he remembered what I had said.

"Thank you, Henry" I said, briskly, Dr. Mrs. Turner, Sunday School teacher, widow, hostess. "You can put it next to the bread."

I squeezed past the people with their empty bowls and walked out into the dining room, my cheeks burning. Someone had brought lemonade and I found a glass and drank some down.

It was then that I heard someone say the word and I turned toward it, eyebrows raised, and saw Ben, Arthur's colleague, who still seemed impossibly young to be a professor, even ten years on. I sidled up to the group that was listening to him. Ben was gesturing with his hands and a girl beside him steadied the bowl in his lap so that it wouldn't fall on the furniture. I silently blessed her and the Scotchgard we had thought to have the sofas sprayed with, for exactly this kind of occasion.

Ben said he would be teaching a course on fracking, public interest had grown to that point. It would be available both for undergrads and for members of the public.

"So, someone could take the course just for interest?" I heard myself ask, and I found my cheeks heating up again.

"Sure," he said, without even taking a breath. "Anyone could."

Before he left, Ben came up to me and asked me about a couple of books Arthur might have had, books he wanted to use for his course. He was apologetic, as if unearthing something he shouldn't. I had spent the better part of the weekend in the study, though, so I didn't think anything of the question, and I remembered seeing one of the books he had mentioned, on Arthur's desk.

He followed me to Arthur's study.

"I'm cleaning it out a bit," I explained as he had to step over piles of books.

"You aren't, you aren't getting rid of these, are you?" he asked, again as delicately as he could. "I mean, if you are, Mrs. Turner, I'm sure the university would be—"

"Oh I know," I said, head tilted sideways, looking for the book. "The letter explaining that arrived not long after the condolence letter."

"Ouch."

"Well, it was only a bit indelicate, but really, I do

understand the motive. And I'm happy to lend you whatever you'd like."

"Thank you," he said, turning to the other side of the room to look through the shelves.

As we hunted for the books—Arthur would have found them in two minutes flat—I thought about the Family Academic Plan that had meant Nick was able to study business at the university, free of charge. Arthur and Nick had always tried to encourage me to take advantage of the Plan but I had always said no. Neither of them could understand it, in ways that were distinctive to them—Arthur because he could not fathom missing learning opportunities, and Nick because "it's saying no to something free, Mom." I had looked through course calendars to appease them but as much as I enjoyed reading, I couldn't exactly see myself enjoying English Literature 1832-1900 or Beowulf or anything else. It was quite enough to be Arthur's wife and Nick's mother. I liked that Nick could bring his friends home and I'd be there, that if Arthur had to travel—geologists had to do that more than you would think—I could man the fort, or go with him, once Nick was grown. My life had never been empty before and I had rarely been particularly curious. The university had sent me all sorts of letters, explaining which benefits I still qualified for as a wife of a deceased professor. The letters were still stacked up somewhere.

"Do you think," I said, turning to him and seeing that he was holding a large stack of books already. "Do you think it would be all right if I took your course?"

"Oh," he said and it annoyed me to see how surprised he looked. "Yes, Mrs. Turner. Of course you could. I think you'd enjoy it."

"How would I register?" I asked. "And what's involved? Oh, and when is it?" I felt like a fool.

"It's a night course, Thursday nights. Starts on the 10th. You can register online."

I nodded. He meant the World Wide Web, which to me was simply the pathway to get to my email account so I could email my son in Singapore. I wasn't about to let Ben Stratton know how illiterate I was. I nodded.

"It's probably free for you," he said.

"Yes," I said. "Ah, here you go. It was this book, wasn't it?" I pulled out a massive encyclopedia of a book and handed it to him. He added it to the bottom of his pile. "You'll let me use it for the required reading, won't you?" I joked.

"Don't worry, Mrs. Turner," he said. "The reading won't be like this. It'll mostly be articles and papers."

Between the lines, I heard him say, *Even you can handle this*, and I felt anger, an I'll-show-them, collide against habitual politeness within me.

"I borrowed a few extras," he said. "I hope you don't mind."

"Go right ahead. I would like them back, though, so I can decide what to do with all his books and papers."

"Daisy?" I heard a voice calling me. It was Cecily.

I held the door open for Ben and we walked down the hall.

Cecily was washing up dishes. I usually shooed her away but tonight, I welcomed her company and her help. I had more to think about than usual—Henry's honey and Ben's course and what it meant to register online. I said goodbye to the last few people and went back to the kitchen.

I had met Cecily when we both returned to the church around the same time, both of us slightly sheepish in the terror that had driven us back, one of us bald and wearing a bandana. Cecily was seven years past her diagnosis now, an official survivor. She had never stopped working at the restaurant the whole way through and they had been so good, giving her days and weeks when she had needed them. Cancer had finally moved down the list by which she defined herself.

"Could you help me with something else instead of the dishes?" I asked her, and she turned around. "I'm thinking about signing up for a course at the university and they say I have to register online. How would I do that?"

She dried her hands on her jeans and I led her to Arthur's old computer and asked dumb questions and wrote down the smart answers on the back of one of Arthur's printouts. I wasn't ready to sign up just yet, but even Ben's condescension and my own embarrassment at being a dinosaur didn't deter me from the idea that this could be a good thing to do.

The next morning I went through the papers and I found the ones from the university, and the Family Academic Plan still applied to spouses and children under the age of 25, even after the demise of the employee. Demise sounded like food going bad.

I turned on the computer and waited for it to warm up,

and then I wasn't sure. I looked at the clock I kept in the kitchen that had the correct time for Nick—he would still be in his office. I picked up the telephone to call him, and then I hesitated. Was I asking him for permission? I hoped not. No. I wouldn't ask him for permission. But what then? I stood up and put away the bowls from last night, poured myself another cup of coffee and went to sit outside on the back porch.

Arthur and I had never moved to live near the campus. We lived on the edge of downtown not far from Ithaca Falls. We had a closet in our house on which we had measured Nick's changing height on the doorframe—that alone made the house one from which I never wanted to move. Arthur had a similar feeling for the shale cliffs in our neighborhood— he liked living in a place where he could see the changes in geological time much more than he would if we lived higher up where the main thing was the view. Neither did we envy those who had to climb the winding roads up the mountainsides through the winter months. Arthur would hold his hand out flat, palm down and explained that where we lived was on the membrane, the webbing between the fingers, with the mountains rising like knuckles just to the south of us and the lake drawing away to the north, leaving behind silt and sand deposits on which the downtown was built. Rain sometimes passed us by, falling on higher elevations, and sometimes got caught between the fingers that were our lakes, a cloud settling between the mountains.

This morning, although the day promised to be hot, the

mountains whispered autumn to me, the sunlight on the trees above me giving the illusion of golden leaves and purple air. I sat and drank my coffee, staring at the canopy of leaves high above us. A mourning dove called hoarsely from beneath my neighbor's eave, breaking open my train of thought.

What indeed? What if I couldn't handle the reading? What if I didn't belong in a class with people younger than my own son? What if they laughed at me? What if I had to do a presentation? What if it was like that terrible art grief group I had attended in the summer? What if—and suddenly I heard Arthur's mother's voice, saying more than once, "If ifs and buts were candy and nuts, we'd all have a merry Christmas." I had not been sure of what she meant when she said it—she was always one with a phrase for an occasion—but it had something to do with not making excuses.

"Of course you're scared," I said aloud. But nothing ventured, nothing gained. Would I call Nick? Would there be any purpose other than permission? If I didn't tell him, I could fail quietly. But Nick never failed quietly—Nick wore his heart on his sleeve and had it broken regularly. It might do Nick good to know I was afraid.

Before I phoned him, I wrote on a printout beside the phone: *Not asking permission.*

"Nick?"

"Mom? Are you all right?"

"I'm fine, I'm fine. You always assume something's wrong."

"But it's the middle of the night there. Why wouldn't I

assume something's wrong?"

"It's seven-thirty," I said.

"Oh crap," he said. "It's later than I thought, then."

"Do you need to go?"

He sighed. "No. I've already missed the meeting I was supposed to be at. So, how are you?"

"I'm well," I said, my stomach jumping. "Actually, I'm a bit nervous."

"You going on a date or something?" He laughed. "Sorry."

I frowned at the phone. "I'm calling to tell you that I'm signing up for a course at the university."

"Good for you. I always told you you should. What are you taking?"

"It's a course on fracking."

"Fracking?"

"It's something new in geology. I think Dad was reading about it before he passed away. It's a way of extracting natural gas from shale rock."

There was a silence. "You don't have to do this, Mom."

This was not the reaction I had expected. "How so?"

"Dad would want you to be your own person. You don't have to study what he studied."

"Oh." I guess it could look like that. Maybe it was. I looked down at the paper. I hadn't registered yet. Why did I want to do this and not Beowulf? It had to do with Arthur and the years I had spent typing all his notes and following him to various places to get samples, sure, but it also had to do with the signs on the roads and with Henry's honey, and with a legacy that had been left to me. "I know I don't have to. But I want to. It's becoming an issue around here and I want to understand it for myself. It isn't just Dad."

His silence was questioning, unconvinced.

"Trust me," I said out loud and I wasn't sure if I was talking to Nick or to myself. I started to doodle on the paper, a chain of daisies. If I could doodle fulltime for the rest of my life, I'm not sure I could cover all the pages left over from Arthur's printouts.

We talked about Nick's work, about his new girlfriend, about how he was playing indoor beach volleyball. I could tell he didn't know what to ask me, and I wasn't sure either, which was one of the reasons I was glad to be taking Ben's course: it gave me something else, a peg for my life once a week, and maybe some homework too.

Arthur's parking pass had finally expired with the start of a new school year. It was a relief to have it done with: a parking pass should not outlive a person. I brought coins and found a spot under a lamp, for it would be dark when I came out, and then I went to the wrong building and very nearly went home again.

I thought of the dreadful grief group early in the summer. I had seen the ads in the paper for years: the grief group that met at the big Presbyterian church near my house. When loneliness began to weigh on me in the weeks after

Arthur's death, I ventured out one Tuesday morning. They greeted me with hugs, although I knew none of them. I was simultaneously repulsed and drawn in by my longing for human touch. And then we went into the gym where large sheets of paper had been taped to the walls around the room. One woman motioned me to a portable coat rack, where people were donning shirts over their clothes.

"This is the grief group?" I had whispered to the woman. She nodded and handed me a smock. It felt like going through security at the airport, where you take off your shoes and jewelry whether you want to or not because someone says you must and because everyone else is and because you want to catch your plane. Against my will and better judgment, I put on a shirt that smelled of cologne, and I swallowed hard before picking up a palette and a brush. I found a spot in front of a piece of paper near the door.

Music I had not paid attention to stopped playing and a small woman in black stood at the center of the room, hands outstretched in welcome.

"Good morning," she said and her voice echoed in the hollowness of the space.

"Good morning," everyone said back to her.

"Flowers grow out of dark moments. Corita Kent. In silence, let your flowers grow. Look inside your heart and let it flow through your hand onto the page. Let us begin."

I lasted fifteen minutes. Fifteen minutes of silence, save the sound of a ticking clock and the faint whine of the fluorescent lights overhead. I looked to my left and watched a woman paint a dark spiral, her face close to the page. I looked to my right, on the other side of the door and another woman was pressing her brush hard against the page, making a series of what looked like duck feet marching, lost, in circles. I lifted the palette and swirled my brush in the paint. It smelled like Nick's kindergarten class, like it should be used for painting happy suns and people with arms and legs coming out of their heads. It felt wholly inadequate for finding, let alone expressing, what was lodged in my heart. I wondered what would happen if I painted nothing, whether paintings would be evaluated or discussed later, how long the interminable silence would last. And then I heard a man sob and I peeled off my paint-shirt and dropped it quietly on the floor behind me, put my palette on top and walked outside into the wave of humidity that was a July morning. I did not look back.

Would this be more of the same?

"Fracking class," I muttered to myself, and it did indeed work as a profanity. Mercifully, I saw Ben walking into a lecture hall and I followed him in and found a seat as quickly as I could and sat there, catching my breath while he adjusted his lectern and started to write on the white board at the front of the class.

I had brought a notebook and I opened it and took a pen from my purse. It had been a long time since I had been in school. Around me, I heard quiet tapping sounds and I turned and saw that I was surrounded by a sea of laptop computers and faces illuminated by the light of their screens. I was in the second row in the seat closest to the door and the lecture hall was built like an amphitheater so I could see the faces around the room, like angels in a choir.

The challenging thing about trying to be a mature student was that it was more than enough for me to try to capture what Ben said, let alone evaluate it. I'm not the world's quickest thinker—I'm a bit of a plodder, frankly—but I'm persistent. I have to let ideas roll around in my mind for a good long time before I decide. People I am more instinctive about and my initial impression tends to be borne out. The young students, though, seemed far more able to assimilate, process and question what Ben had said. I felt like I needed to go home and to read my notes over and to spend time asking myself where I stood on things. Then too I felt frustrated: how was I supposed to know whether what Ben and the readings said was true? I knew Arthur had respected Ben. Ben had started out by saying that this was not a simple issue and that he would try to present all sides of the matter. I knew that he had decided to offer the class because he was concerned that decisions would be made without thought and because it concerned our very own community.

At the end of the class, Ben announced the readings for the following week and I missed the second reading—I found that writing was slower than typing and I envied the students with their computers—as I was still writing down the first. I raised my hand to ask him to repeat the list.

"Sure, Mrs. Turner," he said.

"It's Daisy—Jane," I said.

"Daisy chain?" Ben said and laughed.

I had tried to ask them to call me Jane. My face burned as I wrote down the title of the article he wanted us to read. What had I been thinking?

Outside, the air was mercifully fresh and clear—it felt like fall had arrived and suddenly the embarrassment I had felt slipped away and I held my books to my chest and I felt like I had when I was six years old, coming home after the first day of school, exhilarated to finally be one of the big kids. And just as there had been children in that class who could already read and those who knew the skipping games better than some of us, there was some anxiety about this class— could I keep up?

And then I realized something: I wasn't there to prove anything. I was simply there to learn. That was what it meant to be a mature student, I decided as I drove along the streets that led to my own.

My hand ached from scribbling as I poured hot water for tea when I got home: sore, unused muscles were also signs of a mature student, I thought wryly, and I found arnica cream to rub into the joints. It had been better than the grief group at least.

The next morning, I found the flyers in the recycling box and looked through for something computerish. I had decided that a laptop computer was a good idea. I was a faster typist than writer and the students might be right. I found them all right, but the language might as well have been Greek when I looked at the features. I decided I would go into one of the big box stores, confess my ignorance and hope they wouldn't take advantage of an older lady.

But when I walked in, the store looked bigger from the inside than the outside, all red and black and chrome, high ceilings and shiny objects everywhere. I took a breath, looked at the Help Desk populated by college students and decided to browse first. There had been a time in my life when browsing was a luxury, when I dashed everywhere, but now I had time.

There were models of laptops and I walked around and touched them. I let my fingers play a small tune, tapping a few keys on each one. I lifted one up and was surprised by how small and light it was. I wondered why Arthur had been content with the beast we had at home.

But, how did you choose? I had no idea. I had just turned to go back to the help desk, resigned, when a woman smiled and walked toward me.

"Daisy chain?" she said. "Right?" She was even shorter than me, with a toddler in a sling on her chest, a stud in her nose, and short black hair. "From the fracking class?"

"Oh. Yes," I said.

She held out a hand to me and shook mine firmly. "I'm Carmel. I sat a couple of rows behind you the other night."

"I'm Daisy," I said. "But you knew that. Well, my real name is Jane, but people call me Daisy."

"Which do you prefer?" the young woman asked, head cocked, bright blue eyes on me.

I hadn't been called Jane in more than fifty years. "Either one is fine."

"You know, that's almost never true. But I'm going to take you at your word and I'm going to call you Daisy Jane. Until you tell me which one to choose."

I wasn't sure what to say. The toddler stirred and rescued me. "Who's this?" I asked.

"This is Aurora, my daughter," Carmel said, sliding a hand under the child's bottom. "She fell asleep on the way into town and I managed to keep her asleep while I brought her in here. I need ink for my printer. And neem oil for my trees."

"Oh," I said again, and it was as if this young woman too spoke a different language. I found her mesmerizing. "I'm here to buy a laptop." I looked at her. "My computer is probably older than you. I'm not really sure what I'm looking for."

"Do you want a hand?"

"I'd love it," I said, almost weak with relief. "Thank you. I was about to ask at the help desk but I'm afraid they'd start talking jargon at me."

"I know what you mean," she said. "What do you want your computer to do?"

I found myself explaining Arthur and seeing the fracking signs and deciding to take the course and just wanting to be able to take notes more easily. "I just need a glorified typewriter," I said. "And I'd use it to email my son."

"Okay," she said. "Mac or PC?"

I held my hands up in surrender. "You see?" I said. "You've lost me already."

"Sorry," she said. "Okay." She paused and wrinkled up her

nose. "I guess I should ask: are you more of a visual person or a numbers person?"

I thought about it. "I don't know," I said. "I really want to keep it simple."

"What do you have now?"

That I did know. I had checked before I left. I found the slip of paper I had written it on. "An IBM 386."

"We had one of those when I was growing up," she said. "Okay, they should have something kind of like that."

She led me to a laptop display I had looked at before. "How about this?" she asked.

"What should I be looking for?" I asked.

"I guess, is there anything you don't like. And color."

"Color?"

"This one comes in a variety of colors. See."

In my experience, computers had been gray and black. I had choices of red, green, purple, black and silver.

"I should probably get black," I said.

"You probably shouldn't," she said, and she reminded me of Nick, all mouthy for a good cause. "You want the green one."

"I do?"

"You looked at all of them but you touched the green one."

"It reminded me of a ring I once had," I said. "Exactly that color."

"There you go then."

In less than five minutes, I was handing over my credit card and being handed a flat box.

"Call me," she said. "If you have any questions." And she

wrote her number on the back of her receipt and handed it to me. I watched her climb into a pick-up truck, strap the still-sleeping baby into the back and drive off. I put my laptop in the passenger seat beside me. I was near Buttermilk Falls and I decided to drive in for a few minutes.

Many people had a favorite waterfall—one they would direct guests to, one they would visit time and again, for family picnics or quiet contemplation. I wondered sometimes whether these were people who served meatloaf on Mondays, pork chops every Tuesday—each week's menu a replica of the one before. Because how could I choose? Ithaca Falls was the nearest, the neighborhood falls, the one I had walked to, dazed when the doctor first told me I was pregnant with Nick. Taughannock was the best for a walk; the most beautiful was the falls at Robert Treman but it required careful footing to negotiate the cut-stone stairs. Nick and I used to debate about which stones had been cut by people and which had fallen naturally in straight lines and blocks. Buttermilk Falls had the easiest approach—although one of the hardest climbs—you could see it from the road, could walk across paved pathways to picnic tables at its base, but it was a straight vertical climb to the top, one my knees could no longer take. It was a good drive-in waterfall for me now.

I sat at the base of the falls. I would be tired that night after so many acts of bravery—admitting all I didn't know, reclaiming my long-buried name, buying a lime-green laptop, trusting a woman I'd never met before, following the installation steps and finally going onto the website Ben had given us, the one with the files for the readings—but for now I listened to the constancy of the water tumbling over the rocks and let the purchase settle in me.

3
Corn Chowder

People said I was so kind, that they would feed me one of these days, but I was fed in bits and pieces, scraps of information and knowledge on Wednesday nights. I had learned to see them as providential, these snippets of conversation that came to my ear as I replaced spoons or collected glasses. Not all of the knowledge was deep and profound—I would sometimes hear that strawberries were in season two weeks early, that a circus was coming to town, or that a road would be closed for construction. Sometimes, though, the knowledge was necessary.

I was saved by it when there came a time in each day when I felt as if a wall had risen up in front of me and there was no way forward, save magical solutions like Arthur returning or night suddenly falling hours early so that I could sleep and escape the neverendingness of widowhood and loss. I could not do it at all. In the midst of my panic I suddenly remembered a conversation I had heard on a Wednesday night, marathon runners talking about hitting a wall. I had come closer to listen, wondering whether someone had been injured. Instead, the wall, like mine now, was figurative and at the same time terribly physical.

"It's when you believe you can't put one foot in front of the other, but you keep doing it nonetheless, and then the wall eventually disappears."

I thought of the runner's wall the next time I faced my own, the very next day. Because it came every single day at some point, a stitch in my side, in my heart really, a weariness that said enough was enough and couldn't I rest a bit from the work of grief? The way out is through, the runner had said, and so I did not turn on Oprah this once, did not numb myself with celebrity news. Instead I felt every fiber of my being ache with fatigue and sorrow and I let myself sit in the garden and soak in the pain. And then, eventually, I found my mind drifting to wonder about the flowers, noticing that the Japanese lanterns had emerged, and wondering whether I should pick some for the table, and then aware that the pain had gone, again. I tried hard not to look too closely, in case examination of the wound, poking and prodding it, caused it to break open again.

The next day when the pain came, I was in the kitchen, washing dishes, and this time, I asked myself, "What do you need?" and I decided I needed rest, so I let myself lie down on the sofa, put my feet up in the middle of the day, and I just breathed in and out, missing my husband and letting the weight of my life settle over me, without having to hold myself upright. My mind began to drift into almost dreams and my breathing slowed but then I heard my neighbor outside and I wondered whether she could see me stretched out on the sofa, what she would think if she could, and with self-consciousness roused, the grief was tucked away again. It reminded me of the contractions I had when I was pregnant with Nick. Two solid weeks of useless, intense contractions. I dilated one centimeter in that whole time, contractions that took me off guard every fifteen minutes, causing me to suck in my breath quickly as everything tightened around one small point. What amazed me was not so much the contraction, but the fourteen minutes in between, where everything was restored to complete normalcy. That a wave could take you and take you so hard and then let you drift away afterward, that was what stunned me, both in birth and in grief.

The next morning I woke up early, constricted with sorrow, and I couldn't make myself go through the pain. I decided to walk down by the lake. The days were getting noticeably shorter now but the early-morning sunlight was still bright and warm. I walked out onto the little wooden dock that jutted out into the lake and leaned against the railing, and I watched the ducks. There was a peculiar comfort in small things like ducks. I looked around at the lake and the mountains of Ithaca and wondered how I had ended up here and then I blurred my eyes and traced back the decisions that had brought me here. My mother had been educated at the Emma Willard School in Troy, New York, when her parents sent her there while they traveled. My parents did not travel, not in the same way or to the same degree, but my mother felt that the Emma would be good for me. Decision number one. I boarded there, happily, with other girls for my high school career. Many of the other girls were from New York and so as we approached graduation, they persuaded me to come out at a debutante ball in New York with them, rather than, as my mother had wished, at the Spring Ball at the Cabarrus Country Club where my father had been a member for many years—"so that you could have your cotillion there," my mother said. At first she had refused to come and then she insisted on making my dress—white netting with daisies sewn across the Empire waist.

If I hadn't been at the deb ball there, I wouldn't have met Arthur, who had been dragged along as an escort for his sister, and who was finishing up his Ph.D.

We had been standing side by side on the edge of the room, each watching everything that was going on, and I smelled him before I looked at him, the scent of Old Spice I associated with older men. And then he made a chance remark to me about the whole crazy business of debutantes and I laughed and he looked over at me and realized I was one of them and then he blushed. I think it was his blush that sealed it for me, that and the fact that he then felt he needed to make it up to me and so he fetched me ice cream and champagne and took me out on the dance floor.

The whole purpose of the debutante ball was to introduce young girls to society, which we knew was code for Find a Good Husband. For me, it was as easy as that conversation and that dance. My mother somehow knew his people from somewhere and my friend knew Arthur's sister from grade school, and we all went out for breakfast together the next morning, and Arthur asked if he could call me. My saying yes was yet another of the decisions that brought me to Ithaca.

We were married just before Christmas and I joined Arthur in his little apartment in Chicago. I was almost nineteen years old and I was Dr. Mrs. Turner, or would be as soon as Arthur defended his thesis. It was heady and baffling. I had dated the same boy throughout high school for three years, the brother of one of my friends. Arthur was older and he had nearly three degrees to my none. I can see now in hindsight that I was playing grown up, but when you're eighteen and finished high school, debutante balls, hope chests and homemaking can be extremely seductive. I approached being Arthur's wife—and later, even more, Nick's mother—with all the thoughtfulness and energy that some women put into their careers.

We moved to Ithaca a few years later as part of the groundswell that was the 1970s. The art gallery on the hill was new and avant garde then, and the farmers market was newly established. The college was hiring and hiring. I was never exactly certain whether I was Town or Gown. Certainly people would have seen me as part of the university but while I was always comfortable myself in my choice not to go on to higher learning, I did feel a bit like a mutt among pedigreed dogs.

For more than thirty-nine years, virtually since I had left high school, I had been Arthur's wife and for almost as long

I had shouldered the social obligations that accompanied the role of being the spouse of a professor in a college town. Now, Wednesday nights aside, there were none. The funeral home had been filled with family and what I had thought were friends, but really were colleagues and acquaintances, people for whom the point of connection was really, as it turned out, likely Arthur. So many of Arthur's colleagues were retiring and moving away. There was something about hosting Wednesday nights, too, that kept me at a slight remove from the others —I-thou, hostess-guest—and then so much had been Arthur and Daisy. I thought of that Bible story, the house built on the sand and the one built on the rock, how when the storms came, the foundations were tested. What was most unfortunate was that I discovered this at exactly the time that I needed a friend with whom I could be entirely honest and open.

Throughout the summer, I had looked at people on Wednesday nights, at neighbors, at parishioners at church with lustful eyes, wondering whether there were any with whom I could confide my terrible, crushing loneliness, any I could call late at night when I just needed to hear a voice. Loneliness is an embarrassing kind of condition like hemorrhoids or constipation—something you should know how to prevent, something you should be able to manage. Cecily was my friend, but I wasn't sure I could call her in the middle of the night. I thought about looking up girls I had gone to school with years before and then I paused: they were likely fully embedded in their own lives as much as I had been in mine.

But now I decided I had to find a place within my own life. As I walked home to make soup for the next day—corn chowder—I decided I would make myself sit, I would perch a while on the edge of a conversation, listening rather than circling the room as a good hostess should. I would let Cecily help instead of shooing her away. I would become smaller and everything would go on without my orchestration. I would organize everything ahead of time and there would no doubt be two or three mad dashes to the kitchen, but for the first time in years, I would find a place for myself as a guest in my own home.

At the end of the class, I pushed save and heaved a sigh of relief. It had indeed been much easier to type than to take notes. I was unplugging my little green computer when I saw that someone wanted to get by.

"Sorry," I said, turning my legs to one side in the aisle.

"Daisy Jane. How are you and your laptop doing?"

It was the girl who had helped me at the computer store. Carmen, I thought her name was.

"Carmel," she said, seeing me hesitate. "My mother named me after a mountain in the Bible. Although when you grow up on an apple farm and your name is Carmel, you get Candy Apple quite a bit."

I laughed. "I'll remember your name," I said. "How's your

little one?"

"My brother looks after her on Thursday nights. Woo hoo! It's my big night out on the town. Hey." She stopped and put a hand on my arm. "A bunch of us are going out for drinks. Do you want to join us?"

I had five wholly unplanned days ahead of me—I thought I could pencil this in. "Okay," I said. "Are you sure?"

"Of course," she said. "Do you need a ride?"

"Just directions."

I was fine after dark at the college and in Collegetown, but somehow I felt nervous downtown alone. The Commons was different at night. By day it was bright with musicians, students, tourists, activists and food vendors. At night it glowed and glittered and you had a sense of darkness— that just outside the pools of light it was murkier. Yellow lights fell on fat men as they found stores that sold liquor or adult movies. Police patrolled the Commons, but even they looked vulnerable. Students sat and laughed at outdoor seating outside restaurants where in a month or so it would be too cold and all the tables would be brought inside for the winter. At night all the crunchy granola types had gone home to make granola or to sleep in hemp sheet beds. Night downtown was darker.

I felt darker inside too. Was this pity? How did this work, things like this, like splitting the bill? I knew now how to go out alone but before that, when we had gone out with friends, it had been taken care of for me. I reminded myself that this was what I had wanted but I held my purse close to my side.

I saw Carmel waving wildly from a booth and I waved
back, walking over to join her. I felt like I was in high school
again, high school where it could be lethal to sit at the hip
kids' table. Carmel with her nose ring was hipper than me
in my Hush Puppies and blazer. But when I turned to be
introduced to the others at the table, I was surprised.

She introduced me to a man with a distinctive Amish beard
on his young face, who wore what looked like homemade
clothes. His family had farmed their land for almost a
hundred years. She introduced me to a tattooed man named
Nate who was taking the course because he was opposed to
multinationals and globalization and I don't know what else.
And then there was a woman named Kathy who wore thin
wire-rimmed glasses and who wrote for the paper.

"Everyone, this is Daisy Jane. Her husband was a geology
professor."

"He died five months ago," I said, and then I looked at their
young faces and realized that this was a terrific way to halt
conversation. It was up to me to recover the situation, to be
the mature person, but it was a bit like finding yourself in
water that was too deep and scrambling to get purchase and
realizing that you just couldn't. I looked up at Carmel and
signaled with my eyes for help.

"They serve our cider here," she said. "You should really try
it."

"Cider?" said the man with the tattoos.

"Hard apple cider," she said and I could feel Arthur recede,
and that I was saved, apparently by the numbing effect of

conversation about alcohol. I sat down and I could feel sweat at the back of my knees. As my heart resumed its normal beat, I could hear Carmel speaking again. "My brother takes care of the marketing and I take care of the apples. The rest has to take care of itself."

"That is what it's like for us too," said Amos, the Amish man. "Only we have more brothers and sisters."

"I used to think one was more than enough when I was a kid," Carmel said. "But now I'd clone him pretty happily. Or myself."

"Which is yours?" I asked, looking at the menu.

"Heritage Cidery," she said, looking upside down over the top of my menu. She brought a roughened index finger down the page. "There. If you don't like it, just tell me you do."

I had a glass of the fizzy dry apple cider and I liked it—"half the alcohol of wine and all the cancer-fighting benefits," Carmel proclaimed.

"I thought your brother was the marketer?"

"Everybody has to do marketing to stay afloat," Carmel said.

"That's why the mining rights offers are so tempting," the man with the tattoos said. "They promise to keep the farms safe and the banks away."

"But common sense says—"

And that was how the conversation went—as light as the bubbles in my glass, tart and bright. I sat and listened and so, mostly, did Kathy. She told me that she was auditing the course at the request of her editor, that the paper could see that this was not going to die away quickly, not with foreclosures being what they were and the threat of peak oil growing ever closer.

I was not even tipsy but I felt so stimulated, so overwhelmed by the conversation that after a short while I excused myself, went to the ladies' room and rested my head on the cool metal stall door for a minute. You made one small change—you went to help a friend harvest his honey and you ended up in a bar with the media, the Mennonites, and the activists, drinking sparkling cider after dark. I wondered what Arthur would say. I imagined coming home and Arthur would be there, him smelling the hint of alcohol on my breath and me explaining where I had been and what I had learned. I didn't think he would object, but he would be disturbed, he wouldn't quite recognize his Daisy, he would see that things had changed.

"It's your fault," I mouthed. "You're the one who changed everything. I was fine with things the way they were."

I made myself go back out into the bar and slide in again. I listened as they talked about how the glacial retreat had left behind the best of soils and the proximity to water. It was why there were wineries everywhere and farms and fruits, why we were spoiled rotten at our market. It was a good place to grow good food. Not everywhere was, but this was.

I made myself sit there and watch their bright, angry, hopeful faces, their desire to save the world, and beneath the table, I twisted my wedding ring on my finger.

4
Roasted Red Pepper and Pesto Soup

It was the day after we went to the bar that I first got sick, sick with aching in my marrow, and glands swollen in my throat where I had not known I even had glands.

I had always been healthy. I could only remember a handful of occasions when I had a cold—generally when Nick started a new school and brought home a fresh array of germs. Colds in the Turner household generally meant that I bought Kleenex and made chicken noodle soup, and we ate supper in our pyjamas in front of the television and woke the next morning nearly all better. Nick had compensated for this with a series of visits to the emergency room—I had started to wonder for a while whether the child protective services were going to knock at our door to see whether the sports injuries were actually a front for some abuse. He had broken both his arms on different occasions as well as his collarbone, and had to have a pin put in his left ankle. We owned a pair of crutches that had been Nick's and they were well worn. Even now, more than a dozen years after Nick had left home, I was reluctant to part with them, just in case. When Nick got what I suspected was a concussion, I decided I would wake him every two hours rather than going to the hospital for the second time that month. And that was really all until Arthur's

heart began its irregularities a few years ago. I would go to
the doctor for my annual physical and it was utterly a non-
event. I had hot flashes during menopause—enough to cause
global warming —but that was about it.

Now, half-dizzy, I dragged myself off to my doctor's office,
imagining, as I sat sweating in the waiting room, that soon
Nick would be returning, an orphan. My doctor was casual—
she did a throat swab and had it quickly examined, took my
temperature and blood pressure and shrugged. "Virus," she
said.

"What can you give me for it?" I asked.

She shrugged again. "It just takes time." She prescribed
rest and Advil and liquids. I felt outraged but too shaky to
say anything. I drove home, eyes blurring, wanting someone
to take care of me. There was chowder left over from
Wednesday night I could heat up, and that was all I could
manage. I sat on the kitchen floor and spooned soup into my
mouth and down my sore throat. How could Arthur wake
up, apparently fine, and drop dead two hours later, while I felt
like death and could be sent home to ache? I started to panic,
sure the doctor had missed something, but I had no energy
for that kind of panic. I left my door unlocked that night, in
case someone had to get in to help me.

By the next morning I was better enough to make myself
something to eat, but four days later, my ear began to ache,
enough to wake me in the night.

"Sometimes grief takes a physical toll," my doctor said when
I went in insisting on an explanation. It was an ear infection.

"But I've never been sick."

"Your body is telling you to rest."

I dragged myself through the Wednesday supper, throwing together roasted red peppers and pesto from the freezer, unable to taste it well enough to even know if it was too salty. I told Ben I wouldn't be at class the next night, feeling desperately guilty, but he only nodded.

When Henry learned that the chief recurring symptom I had was a throat like cut glass, he showed up the next morning with a jar of buckwheat honey and a plastic spoon, and handed them to me, insisting I take my medicine. I was in my housecoat and slippers, my pockets filled with balled-up tissues. I pulled my housecoat tighter at the neck, but beyond that, I didn't have the will to care.

"There's antibacterial properties in honey," he said. "And antiviral and antifungal. People used to think it was nectar from the gods."

I took a large spoonful of honey—I would have swigged bleach by this point if I had thought it would help—and let it dissolve on my tongue while he talked. The honey coated my mouth thickly and made me thirsty so that I almost couldn't speak.

"Do you have lemons?" he asked. I shook my head. "Lemon juice?"

"Fridge," I managed to say.

"May I?" he asked, coming into my house.

He had of course been there each Wednesday for years, but it was strange being there with him on his own, strange that he could find his way around my kitchen, perhaps more than Arthur ever had. I sat at the table and watched Henry fill the kettle with water. Arthur had grown up in a family with a housekeeper and he had learned at an early age that the kitchen was her domain. Old habits had died hard with Arthur. Most nights, he had waited in the dining room for me, a magician, to present—ta da!—that night's dinner.

As I directed Henry to where I kept the mugs, I realized it could not be so at his house, not with Jane being sick. Maybe he had been the kind of man who waited for his dinner too, but he was no longer that man. He was a man who really could conjure food—could bring honey out of the hive. It made me think of Samson and his riddle—out of the eater came something to eat, out of the strong came something sweet. No one had been able to solve Samson's riddle until his wife had tricked it out of him, out of loyalty not to him.

I wondered if I was feverish again. Certainly I had not heard that story in years, not since I had returned to church. It had been one of the stories I had learned as a child, one of the complicated stories like David and Bathsheba that made me wonder at the disconnect between the tameness of the church and the wildness of the Bible. I remember wondering whether no one else got it, whether no one else was really listening to the stories.

Henry held a mug out to me, steaming. I took it and took a sip that burned my throat.

"Lemon juice, cayenne and honey—in hot water," he said, pulling out another chair at the table. Pulling out Arthur's chair and sitting in it. "It was what my mother gave us when we were small and sick. Drink it."

I could do what I was told to do. Which was partly why all the talk of virus and waiting it out and resting was so hard on me. Because I was a doer, I was someone who was unaccustomed to being alone, unaccustomed to being ill, to being quiet, to resting. Tell me to drink this magic potion and I would obey.

"Actually," he said as I sipped, "my mother didn't add cayenne. Lee Henshall told me that she always added it. She added garlic too, but I've never tried that."

The startling thing was that it worked. Henry left the jar of buckwheat and I finished it off, dark and thick, mixed with lemon juice, so that my stomach started to ache with the sweetness and the acidity of it, but within three days of drinking it, I was well again.

I thanked Henry on Wednesday night when he came again, and a look crossed his face. I knew he had started the hive for Jane, hoping it could make her well; while he had intended that it would have a good effect on me too, the fact that it had, I had to think, caused him some degree of pain.

But he winked and smiled. "I'll be your pusher, Daisy," he said. "I'll bring you the good stuff." I knew he would be true to his word, showing up with small jars each week, not letting me pay him anything.

I felt uneasy when I went to class on Thursday night, that perhaps Ben would require a doctor's note I didn't have, but no one seemed to have noticed. I couldn't tell, though, whether my vague confusion came from residual sickness, having missed a class or not being up for the challenge of being a student.

Ben talked about the mechanics of fracking. To me, it sounded neutral, a how-to, but there was a lot of emotion in the students—anger and outrage. Either people saw fracking as progress, something that might save them from the very real threat of foreclosure, or they saw it as something that might cause a very real threat to our water. I thought about the water I had drunk at Henry's cottage, cool, fresh, unfiltered lakewater. There weren't many places where you could do that.

Carmel was clearly against fracking. She sat beside me in class and I typed diligently away, at every word Ben said or anyone else in class said. My notes might as well have been a transcription. Not Carmel. She brought a laptop, but she made few notes. Instead she banged away at the keyboard when she did type, and raised her hand on a regular basis. I had already come to know that she was the fourth generation on her family apple farm, that she was the first generation organic since her great grandfather, that apples were one of the most chemical-sensitive crops you could grow, that she was part of a new coalition opposing fracking and that she was mostly in the class to evangelize.

At the end of the class, she turned to me and smiled with a dimple that had been absent throughout the lecture. "Daisy Jane. How's your laptop? Is it working for you?"

I loved my laptop. It was mine and it was lovely. I dusted its screen every time I used it, kept its battery humming, found a case for it, and it made me happier than any possession I could remember.

"Yes," I said. "It's working so well. Thank you."

I asked Carmel whether I could borrow her notes from the previous week. She reached into her pocket, found a piece of paper and a pen, and scribbled something on the top of the paper. "That's my email address—email me and I'll send you the notes. Such as they are. Good thing you didn't need notes from today's class. I was tired and mad."

"I noticed the mad part," I said.

"Sorry. No, I'm not sorry. If you can't get mad about something like this, what can you get mad at?" If she was this mad about clinical descriptions of the hydraulic fracturing process and its history, what would she be like when the fracking company came in to promote its practices? "Hey, Daisy Jane, a bunch of us are going to start with a road trip to Pennsylvania to protest fracking there in a couple of weeks. Want to join us?"

How could I tell her the scope and shape of my life? How would I tell her that it was small and measured, safe and proper? It occurred to me that if you knew your life was safe and small, it was too small and too safe, that people never chose to live small. Some people did live small lives but perhaps that was all they were capable of. When you could see the horizons, the edges, was it not a prison of a sort?

"Tell me more about it," I said.

Look at me, I wanted to say. I know how to make soup for a

crowd. I know how to type papers for my husband. Those are my skills. I'm figuring out the rest as I go. Protester is not on my resume.

And then I remembered that it was. I remembered the year at Nick's school and how I had stood before the school board, knees shaking, to talk about a breakfast program. Nick had told me about a girl in his class who had fainted and it turned out she hadn't eaten in two days. I went to see his teacher, appalled, and it turned out there was more than one kid who came to school hungry. In Ithaca. I didn't think twice about speaking up. I said I would make sure every kid in our school was properly fed to start the day. It choked me, feeding oatmeal to Nick and knowing that he had friends who were drinking water to fill their stomachs in the morning. I was mad then, mad enough to do something. And that had resulted in a breakfast program and higher average grades for the school in the state statistics.

"It's a kind of blockade," she said. "Very peaceful. We hope anyhow."

"I'll think about it," I said.

"Hey, is that your son?" Carmel asked, looking at the picture on my screen, a man surfing a huge curl of a wave.

"Oh no," I said. "That came with the computer."

"You can change that, you know."

I looked at the slip of paper later as I prepared to email her: it was a gas station receipt. Since the course had started, every time I drove my car, I felt complicit in the need for drilling. I wondered whether Carmel did too. I didn't want to ask.

On Saturday, before I went to the market, I walked up to the Commons, my heart in my throat, to sign up for the road trip to Pennsylvania. You could always count on Daisy to help out. I walked past a man on the Commons, not sure whether he wore a phone in his ear or was talking to himself. I heard him say night—or was it knight?—and poetry, and somehow, whether he was talking to himself or not, I lost my fear of him. I went into the secondhand bookstore and up the stairs, past the café with skulls smiling at me, and then I sighed with relief: Carmel had said that the anti-fracking group had a desk in the office at the front of the second floor but the door was closed and barred.

At the market I saw a potter selling little bee skeps—the little woven hives—made out of clay, with lids and one of those wooden devices for scooping honey out of the jar. I picked one up—that was when she introduced me to the word skep—and then put it down quickly, blushing. Why would I presume that the honey had an endless supply? This was no promised land. I walked on and collected grapes, sprays of sage and the first squash of the season. And then I walked past a stand selling honey, and stopped. I turned back and there were samples.

I thought to myself: you can get honey anytime you like. It doesn't have to be Henry's honey. You can buy a little beehive if you want one.

There were open jars of honey—with late-season wasps threatening them—and a jar of popsicle sticks. You could dip a stick in any of the honeys you liked, sampling them. My first instinct was to try the one that looked like the one I had been eating every day—but it was basswood and had a sourness to it that I hadn't expected. The clover honey had a tang to it like flowers and I thought I might like it in tea. I tried every one of the honeys, collecting a handful of used popsicle sticks as I went, but I felt like Goldilocks where none was just right.

There were little signs on the poles at the back of the booth. I read as I sampled. One said that local honey was good for allergies because it exposed you to the allergens in a way that transformed them. That, it said, was why it was good to buy local. Your body knew the taste of its land. It knew what it needed.

I knew that what I needed was to not be dependent on a single source of honey. I thought that the clover would taste good in tea.

"Do you carry buckwheat?" I asked the young girl who took my money.

She shook her head. "We get it late in the season," she said. "And it goes quick."

There was a scattering of leaves on the ground, not many but enough to signal that fall was really here. Market stalls were decorated with corn stalks and straw bales and there was even the occasional early pumpkin or gourd. I could see the geese were still on the lake beyond the pavilion.

"Daisy! How are you?"

I turned. It was my neighbors, Peg and Bill Parsons. Sometimes I would tell Arthur I was going to the market to pick up a few things and it would be hours later when I returned; he would find it hard to believe I hadn't been elsewhere. There were just that many people to bump into at the market.

"I'm well. How are you?"

"It's wonderful to see you out and about, Daisy," Peg said, brightly, as if I had been locked away in seclusion. "Is there anything we can do for you?"

I thought quickly. "Actually, maybe there is. Seeing leaves on the ground today makes me think that I need to find a boy to rake my leaves soon. Who does yours for you?"

"The Bells' son. Luke. Lives across the street from us," Bill said. "What are you doing about your eaves?"

"My eaves?"

"You need to clear those troughs after the leaves fall or you'll have trouble. I could do them for you when I do ours."

I hadn't even known eavestroughs needed cleaning. I cleaned the inside of the house; that was my domain. I stacked the printouts from the research. I cooked the meals. I typed Arthur's notes. I took the car to the shop for oil changes. I paid the bills and did the banking. Arthur had fixed things, primarily, kept things going. People had said to me that couples of our generation settled into our roles easily, and then, when one spouse died there was complete confusion. One night in the summer, there had been a storm and a fuse blew. I called Nick, woke him in the middle of the night, and he directed me to the basement, to the fuse box. I had lived in the house for thirty-six years, had done my laundry in the very same room, and I had never before even noticed the fuse box, let alone opened it. And the fuses were lovely glass knobs. I had gone to the hardware store the next day, the one on Main, and wandered the aisles, touching the fuses, turning away help until I had finished enjoying them. They reminded me of the glass museum in Corning, the one I loved and Arthur hated. I kept the burned-out one on the kitchen window ledge afterwards, partly for its beauty and partly out of wonder for the things I did not know. Which were many. And now it was eaves.

"I would be so grateful," I said and I smiled at him. Out of the corner of my eye, I saw Peg's hand snake around her husband's arm, possessively, I thought. As if my willingness to borrow her husband for an hour meant I was a threat. I had no idea how to defuse that kind of tension.

"We need some wine for that dinner we're going to," Peg said. "We'll see you soon, Daisy."

"Yes," I said and I felt shaky and walked out to the end of the dock and took deep breaths. I thought about Carmel's notes from the class I had missed, the second half of Ben's lecture on the formation of the Marcellus Shale, the rock on which the whole Eastern Seaboard stood. It was similar to a lecture Arthur had given, one I knew well. Carmel's notes had been sketchy, stream-of-consciousness, almost like poetry, but one phrase stood out to me—"the long slow

underwater avalanche." I knew from typing for Arthur what
she meant, the millions of years it had taken for the shale
to form, mountains rising and falling, mud and organic
matter slowly sinking in water so dense it was nearly without
oxygen. But the phrase had stuck with me like a mantra. I
stood at the end of the dock and breathed the words: the long
slow underwater avalanche. And then, eventually, I gathered
myself together—I had a Sunday School lesson to prepare for
the next day—and headed back through the market toward
home.

I looked again at the bee skeps as I passed. They were
darling. I hadn't bought anything new for the kitchen in
years and years—other than a new garlic press when mine
collapsed—and certainly nothing decorative. But something
in me said no to this, that it would somehow give more place
to honey in my life than I was ready for.

When I got home, I made myself a cup of tea and added
a spoonful of the pale gold market honey. I was still adding
honey to my tea, although for years I had drunk it clear
and black. It felt like some sort of talisman against illness,
something I really should do. This honey, though, made it
taste different somehow, almost like a flavored tea. I finished
it but I wasn't sure about it. I also didn't want to hurt Henry's
feelings, so I hid the clover honey behind the oats in my
cupboard and tried to forget that it was there.

5
Borscht

I never felt that any conversation on a Wednesday night was private or even exclusive. Occasionally I found a couple on the back steps or upstairs in a hallway in an intense conversation but generally Wednesday night talk was fluid, wide-ranging and open to newcomers.

"You talking about Saturday's game?" Father Jim said, pulling up a footstool. "Unbelievable." Father Jim knew about football, knew what not to say to a person in pain, and knew how to give a homily—his homilies reminded me of a lump of pesto dropped into a soup, something that gradually released its flavor into the whole. Arthur would never go to church with me, but he liked Father Jim who came on Wednesday nights when he could, and so it was Father Jim who took Arthur's service although we held it at the university chapel rather than at Immaculate Conception. It was Father Jim who had delivered the cards from my Sunday School class after Arthur died and who had asked me later whether I was ready to start teaching the third-grade girls again.

I listened as Henry explained that he and Jane had had the best seats in the house to judge the play in question. Sports had never been a passion for Arthur or for me; we were never sure where Nick got his fondness and aptitude for it. I had learned the rules of many sports, cheering on the sidelines, but not enough for it to translate into a love of any game itself.

I liked seeing my guests happy; it made me feel successful but more than that, I found that happiness was infectious. It pleased me inordinately to watch Henry laugh over precarious bowls of rich borscht. His hair was silver but his face was tanned without being weathered. It seemed to glow with good health as he gestured.

"Jane hadn't been to a game in three years," he explained. "Too hard on her to walk that kind of a distance. Then I was at a game early on this year and I noticed a man in a wheelchair being brought in and I realized that the wheelchair area had the best view of the field. I persuaded Jane she had to do it at least once, and the weather was fine on Saturday, so there we were, smack behind the Big Red's 40-yard line."

He looked up and his shining eyes met mine. "First time we ever felt like her sickness gave us an advantage."

Something high in my gut ached with a kind of melancholy and I could not say exactly why. Was it the smallness of the consolation or the sweetness of being able to find a silver lining, a spouse still there? It was mostly little things I missed; the big ones I could steel myself for, but it was small things—I dreaded sending out Christmas cards. It had been a shift to take Nick's name off the card and now my name would stand alone. Who could say what things were big and which were small, really?

From what he had told me of Jane, the Saturday excursion would probably still be taking a toll on her weakened, shaking body, but it had been a small break that I had no doubt was worth the cost. The ache I felt might be jealousy, I realized, and that was all the self-awareness I could bear.

As I walked back to the kitchen, I tucked away in my head that football made Henry come to life. I was very glad for him. For him and Jane.

Geology was a slow, slow process, I thought, as I sat in line on the highway, waiting for a construction delay, looking at the mountains around me with new eyes. I tried to imagine the area covered in a sheet of ice and then the slow receding of the glaciers, dragging deposits of rock slowly and unevenly across the land as they melted. Maybe the slowness of geology was why fracking upset people.

Cars were coming at us from the other side for ten minutes before it was our turn and we began to inch forward on the rough road. I watched the leaves on the mountains on either side of us, gladder than glad once again that I lived in this place. There was something deeply satisfying about the reds of autumn and some years were better than others. This was not the best year—maybe the real best years were enhanced by memory—but there were stands of sugar maple that were brilliant in the morning sunshine on the mountains. I was glad for the slowness of traffic so I could enjoy them.

The roads were busier than usual—it was Canadian Thanksgiving weekend and we had lots of tourists from the north coming down. People came in waves—there was usually a quiet month in May when the majority of students were out of school and before the tourists really arrived in earnest around the time of the Festival. A summer of strangers walking the streets and trails. And then, as they left, the students returned and the grocery store was emptied, invariably, of peanut butter. Finally, this last hurrah of tourists at Canadian Thanksgiving. After the leaves fell and the students were deeply immersed in their studies, life would settle down for another winter.

I was driving out to Carmel's farm to see a dog, to pick apples and to have lunch.

"My dog had pups this summer," she had said at class on Thursday. Ben had been giving the history of the environmental movement: Carmel had been calmer. "I've been able to find a home for all but one of them. I've asked everyone I know if they're interested and I can't find a home for him. I'm not asking you to take him, but I wondered if you knew anyone."

I had no idea who would want a dog. I had always been a cat person.

"This is him," Carmel said, holding her phone out to me. I looked at the photo—all brown eyes and black nose, sniffing at the camera. "Ringo." My favorite of the Beatles. "Someone already took Paul and John and George is going on the weekend. That leaves Ringo."

"What breed is he?" I asked.

"Well, my dog is mostly a yellow Lab and I've seen what I think was an Irish setter running through the trees in the orchard, looking pretty proud of himself, so I think that's what they are. Mostly. Did you want to come and see him?"

And I had agreed. Her place was south of town in the direction of New York City. I saw a sign that gave the distance—210 miles. There was absolutely nothing stopping me from driving all day and ending up in Times Square. Other than a visit to a friend. Somehow this made me inordinately glad.

I always feel protected living in the valley of the town as I do, but I also find myself breathing more deeply, opening up as I drive out of town and into the hills. My ears pop as I ascend and descend, but once up high, I love looking down at my town, its lights clustered at the lake's end at night.

The best land for grapes, I had been told, was directly on the limestone ridges beside the lakes, but apples might be different. Carmel had told me to get to the little town and turn right at the stop sign and then turn at the third laneway on the left. There was a whitewashed, hand-lettered sign at the gate that read Heritage Apples and Cidery. I drove up the laneway, which was paved but splintered by grass and wildflowers that had managed to break through the asphalt. The lane was flanked by straight rows of trees. I opened the window and I could smell the scent of rotting apples and I could almost hear the buzz of insects. At the end were two farmhouses, one old and the other a small bungalow cottage, a barn and a small garage-like shed with bushel baskets piled out front. I parked the car in front of the shed, which had a sign saying OPEN in the window.

I walked inside the shed and I breathed in. It smelled of old wood, seasoned, and years of apples, some of which lay quietly in large wooden crates around the perimeter. The room was cooler than the air outside and it reminded me suddenly of visiting my granddaddy's house when I was a little girl and being sent to the cellar to get something. I closed my eyes at the memory and inhaled. And then I heard noise outside and stepped back out. Carmel, in jeans and rubber boots, was coming across the yard from the small bungalow.

"You're here," she said. "Can I show you around?"

"Of course," I said. "Where's Aurora?"

"Watching cartoons with my dad. Eating sugar and smoking a cigar." She laughed. "Okay, probably not the cigar, but let's just say my dad balances out my organic, free-range child raising."

We walked through long grass between rows of trees to a small wire enclosure. I could hear the barking before we got there. A big yellow Lab lay dozing in the sunshine, while a small dog climbed on top of her to try to get to us.

"There's Ringo," Carmel said. "Do you want to meet him?"

Suddenly I remembered the time we had the class gerbil for the weekend, the terror of responsibility I felt. The eyes were too trusting. I thought maybe I could get a cat again, but a puppy felt overwhelming. And yet, I had said I would try. Carmel found a lead and put it around the puppy's neck. She opened the gate and the pup pulled her along, sniffing at everything. She handed the lead to me and patted her hand twice on her thigh. The old mother dog rose to her feet and followed her. Carmel scratched her dog behind her ears. "This is Marilyn," she said. I put the back of my hand out for the big dog to sniff with her wet nose, and the puppy reached up to chew on my fingers. I started. I was a cat person.

"I thought I'd show you the apples and we can bring the dogs along. Give you a chance to get to know Ringo." I nodded and bent my elbow so my arm would have some give the next time the pup decided to lunge at something.

Carmel batted at an insect. "Stupid crazy wasps," she said. "They're just drunk at this time of year. Mean drunk too. But they have great taste in apples. Here," she said, reaching into the branches of a tree and pulling off a pale yellow apple. She reached into her pocket and took out a pocket knife, made an incision in the apple and handed me a slice. "This is one of my favorites."

It was smooth as butter, almost as smooth as a ripe pear and its sweetness filled my mouth. She saw me smile.

"Golden Delicious?" I asked.

"Daisy Jane," she said, hands on hips, knife still pointing outward. "I believe you need an education in apples if you think that was a Golden. We grow nearly thirty kinds of apples here, none of which you can pick up in a Walmart."

"Thirty?"

"You'd be surprised," she said, walking ahead to a different row and pulling a tiny cherry-red apple off the tree. The puppy tried to jump for the apple as she cut a slice and handed it to me. It was tart enough to make my mouth pucker. "Sorry," she said. "Too sour?" She threw the uneaten parts of the apple overhand and they landed with a clunk in a large wooden bin. I was ready this time for Ringo to try to run after it. "Trevor and I can use those for cider still," she said.

"Trevor?"

"My brother. He lives in the big house with my dad."

We walked up the hill, sampling apples as we went. The good part about holding the dog on the leash was that he was like one of those moving sidewalks in an airport, the kind that help you move along just a bit more quickly. I could hold his leash and get half-pulled up the hill. She made me smell one of the apples and it had a powdery-sweet smell. "Roses," she said. "Don't you think? Everyone says roses." She pointed at another tree. "That one is awful eating for months. It won't be good until at least Christmas. I'm not going to subject you to a sample of it. Although if you want to take some and keep them, you'll see what I mean."

"What's the system?" I asked. "I assumed there would be rows of one kind and rows of another."

"Apple trees need to be pollinated by other types of apple trees," she said. "So, we have rows of one kind of tree, but we intersperse them with other kinds for that reason. I have the chart my great-grandfather made when he first planted the trees."

"Johnny Appleseed?" I joked.

"If you knew how many Johnny Appleseeds there really were," she said. "It was one positive thing we brought to the native people. Didn't exactly balance out smallpox and taking their land, but it was a decent gift."

We reached the top of the ridge. "Look," she said, and I turned and looked and apple trees spread out below us like a skirt billowing in the wind. Far below in the distance, I could see Cayuga Lake, a sliver of blue between waves of color.

"It's beautiful," I said, inadequately.

"I will fight for this," she said quietly, "with everything I have."

I stood and looked at the view. I could see the occasional white wind turbine slicing through the air and I knew people had stood against that too, had worried they caused headaches and cancer. I didn't like the look of them but I liked the idea of harnessing the wind, just as they captured the power of the water at Niagara. This was different, I thought. It was probably different.

"I keep thinking about what I'll say to Aurora someday when she's a rebellious teenager and she thinks the whole world is going to shit and it's all the fault of the generation before. What if I say, yeah, I just let it happen. That's what I can't live with. That. Killing the water my trees drink up and killing the future for my baby."

She smiled wryly. "But they'll fight for it too." She shook her head. "Do you still have space for lunch?"

I didn't but I followed her back down the hill. We put the dogs back in their pen and I think I sighed.

"Not for you?" she said with a smile.

I shook my head. "It feels like a lot. He's very sweet but—"

"No pressure, Daisy Jane," she said. "Come on. Let's go get the baby." We walked up the steps to the front door of the farmhouse. She knocked and opened the door. "Dad?" she said.

A man came to the door carrying a jam-faced toddler. Aurora leaped into her mother's arms. I leaned against the porch railing, my knee sore from the climb up the hill.

"Thanks, Dad," she said. "Oh, this is my friend, Daisy Jane. From my class."

He held out a hand and it was a little sticky, but his smile was warm and I saw where Carmel had gotten her dimples. He was about my age, or possibly even younger. "Bob. Pleased to meet you. So you're one of the fracktivists?"

I hadn't heard the term before and I wasn't sure whether he had coined the word or not but it reminded me that I had not yet gone back to sign up for the road trip. "I'm learning," I said, wondering whether I had missed the trip.

Carmel looked outside. "Trevor's not back yet?"

"Market day," Bob said.

Carmel shook her head. "Of course. At this time of year, every day blends into the next. Did you want lunch, Dad?"

"We've been eating all morning," Bob said. "Peanut here probably won't need lunch either."

Carmel gave him a look. I remembered what grandparents

could do. "OK," she said. "Thanks, Dad."

"It looking good?" he asked, holding the door open with his foot.

"You can try some tonight when it's done," she said.

"Cider," she explained to me as we walked to her house next door. "I spent the morning crushing apples and getting the press started for the year."

When I left, it was with a cardboard box filled with a variety of apples and a bottle of hard cider tucked into the side. And a wet kiss from a sleepy Aurora.

"So, there's still time to sign up for the Pennsylvania trip?"

"Absolutely," she said. "And you're sure about the puppy? Just kidding—but if you hear about someone, let me know."

"I do a dinner on Wednesday nights," I said. "I could ask there. Actually, you should come sometime—bring Aurora."

"That's so nice of you, Daisy Jane. Maybe I will."

"And thank you."

"Oh, I almost forgot. You know Amos from class?" Amos the Amish. Yes. "They offered his family $73,000 for drilling rights yesterday." She shook her head. "Who says no to winning the lottery? And yet, what happens if we say yes. What the hell happens?"

I drove off with that sour taste in my mouth after a sweet morning. I opened the window and I drove up and down hills and back roads. The fracking signs had proliferated and spread; there were more of them than political signs in an election year.

I stopped across from a small farm stand on the side of the

road and there was a tin can with a slot in it and bouquets of colorful asters in mason jars. I crossed the road. I felt like I wanted to bring a bit of the beauty back into town with me. It was hard to choose among the bouquets but I found one that reminded me of the leaves—purples and reds and yellows. I had folded my two dollar bills and put them in the slot and was waiting to cross the road again to my car when a man came up the rise, jogging. He staggered to a stop in front of me.

"Daisy," he said, and it was Henry, drenched in sweat in shorts and a gray shirt. "What are you doing here?"

"I was visiting a friend's farm," I said. "I'm just on my way back but it was such a beautiful day, I didn't want to rush."

"The leaves will be gone soon," he said. "I always loved working at this time of year."

"Working?" I said, and another car sped past.

"I was a lineman for thirty-three years," he said. "Hydro poles, repair, that kind of thing. Fall was my favorite time of year."

I nodded. I had heard him say before that he was a lineman, but I had never thought to wonder what that meant, what he actually did. If anything, I had thought he worked on the railways.

"Climb up a pole and you can see for miles," he said.

"What do linemen do, anyhow?"

"Did you ever learn about electrical circuits in high school?"

I thought back to the Emma and the physics classes

where we had to draw diagrams and test them, and one girl throwing fits because she knew someone who had once been electrocuted. I nodded.

"We make the circuits work so that people don't even notice we're there. Figure out where the problems are and anticipate them if you can. It's scaling poles and hiding wires."

"Like a superhero."

"I loved my job," he said. "What I loved most was that you knew you could die if you didn't pay attention and so you gave yourself over to it completely. I haven't really found anything else to replace it."

"What about your bees?" I asked.

He shook his head. "I swear to God I thought beekeeping was stable work and it was until colonies started collapsing a few years ago. So far, there hasn't been any colony collapse in this area. But it's made me think that perhaps nothing is safe anywhere. And when it gets bad, I diagram circuits in my head."

I put my hand on his arm briefly and gave it a squeeze. Two cars passed in opposite directions, swirling wind at my skirt. I clutched it with my free hand and looked down at the flowers.

"You should get some for Jane," I said. "They're only two dollars."

"Didn't bring my wallet," he said.

"I could lend you some money," I said, although all I had left was a twenty.

He shook his head. "You don't happen to have any water

with you, do you? It's warmer than I thought it was."

"I'm sorry," I said. "But I do have a box of apples in the car. Would you like an apple?"

He put a hand in the small of my back, his fingers lightly touching my blouse, as we waited for a space in the traffic. His fingers were hot and I could almost feel his pulse throb in them.

I opened the trunk of my car. "Oh," I said. "I do have cider, but it's hard cider. You don't want that, do you?"

He laughed. "I think I'd better not. I stagger badly enough as it is and there's a lot of traffic along here today. As much as I'd love a drink, I'd better not. "

"Look at all these different kinds of apples," I said. "Carmel grows heritage varieties. She gave me a tour today. You probably want something tart."

"Juicy," he said.

I tried to remember but there were so many. I found one that was freckled and smooth at the same time. "How about this one?"

He took a bite that was almost half the apple. "Perfect," he said, juice at the sides of his mouth. "What kind is it?"

"A red apple," I said. "I'm pretty sure it's a red one."

"I'm lucky to know an expert," he said.

"Are you sure," I said, "about the flowers? I could drop some off to Jane."

He swallowed and took another bite and chewed and swallowed again before he spoke. "She has no sense of smell anymore," he said. "Flowers only taunt her, she says."

"I'm sorry," I said. "Asters don't really have a strong scent anyhow."

"She wouldn't believe me," he said. He took one last bite and threw the core far into the field beside us.

A car passed us and another and I was glad of the noise, for a pause before speaking.

"I'm sorry it's so hard," I said. Henry would know the runner's wall.

"The doctors told us most people live with MS just fine, that with exercise and reduced stress, she'd probably only notice occasional symptoms between flare-ups." He raised his toe off the ground and stretched his calf so hard I thought the muscles would snap. "But some people don't get lucky that way."

"Are you heading up to the lake?" I asked. "Did you need a lift?"

He shook his head. "Thanks but no. I need the exercise."

"Do you want another apple?"

"What do you recommend?"

I cocked my head and smiled as if considering a good apple for a good man. I remembered one. Carmel had given me one with a big stem on it so I could remember its name. "This is a Blacktwig," I said. He looked at me like I was making it up. "It is!"

He took the apple from my hand and there was one extra beat when I thought of Eve and all the trouble that had fallen out from that apple.

"Thank you," he said and he opened the car door and

closed it behind me, keeping his hand on the open window as we said our goodbyes.

As I waited for a break in traffic, I watched him grow smaller in my rearview mirror and then I drove down the hill and he was gone from sight.

6
Apple-Cheddar-Onion Soup

I had the strangest sensation that perhaps the house had sighed or swayed, just a little. I had heard about earthquakes before, how terrifying it was for people in them, precisely because they could not get to a safe place, that even their homes were moving, that even if they went outside, things still shook. This was not like that. It was small and gentle and had I not been standing in the kitchen, had I not heard a book fall off the shelf in the study upstairs, I think I would have thought I had just swayed a little myself. But I didn't call it earthquake to myself. I called it odd, and promptly forgot about it until that night. It was a bit like the Cuban Missile Crisis when I knew about communism and all that, but somehow, my own life seemed more important and the bigger event, the one that rocked the world, didn't exactly register with me. So it was with the earthquake.

The class was that night and the students took over. Carmel was one of those leading the charge. Ben sat at the front of the room and took questions about whether fracking could cause earthquakes. It was then that I named what had happened. Earthquake. The gas that could be fracked had accumulated over long years, millions of years, but the shale would be cracked like a nut and then the gas siphoned off before it seeped away. The long slow avalanche and then the world changed in a moment.

I thought back to the tsunami that hit the Pacific the year Nick moved to Singapore. It was massive, of course, but even though they were so close, Singapore felt precisely nothing. The way the earthquake hit the tsunami made all the difference—the force released just happened to go in other directions and my son was fine. Arthur said it that way—*it just happened to go in other directions*, but it was that event that made me return to church after all those years away.

This one, Carmel insisted, was not an act of God, but an act of man. I was pretty sure that Carmel's language around that was deliberate—that by man she meant Dick Cheney and his crew, not humankind. She meant men.

"Could it really do that?" I asked.

Ben shrugged, but he nodded. "Technically, it could. Technically, we don't know what it takes to destabilize rock."

I remembered hearing that some boats rode the tsunami in the Pacific, that when the wave hit the land it went inland for miles, but that out on the open ocean, it only raised and lowered boats. If you were already adrift, you didn't feel the force of the wave, you rode it. I wished that was how it always was.

"I think maybe we do know," I said.

Ben looked at me, startled, as I expressed my opinion.

Until then, it had been a big thing for me to even go to class, to do the readings, to listen as other people argued. But I realized too that there was something familiar about it—being an observer, listening from the periphery. It had felt big but it hadn't really been big, hadn't really been the earthquake, only the tremors. Speaking up, having an opinion was a different matter. Expressing that opinion shifted the balance from Daisy to Jane, from the hostess to the—what? I didn't know what. It felt very new and raw. I remembered when the feminist movement took hold. *The Feminist Mystique* came out around the time I became a teenager. I remembered older girls in my school making different choices because of it, but when you're called Daisy, there is a strong expectation that you will bloom and be pretty, and I didn't really have the resources, internal or external, to do otherwise.

My daddy had placed the hand I draped over his arm into Arthur's and that had been that.

As I drove home, a spark of light caught my eye. I looked for it again, and there, suspended high above the street, was a man in a small metal bucket that looked like a seat from a ferris wheel. Another was scaling a pole across the street, while yet another held up traffic as the two men suspended wires high across the road. Maybe something had come loose in the earthquake.

I wondered how someone decided to become a lineman. You needed to be willing to work outdoors, I thought, and you couldn't be too afraid of heights. Beyond that, I wasn't sure what was involved.

I wasn't sure how someone decided to become an activist either but I felt restless after the class and I decided to go for a walk. The evening was warm and as soft as a kiss—I didn't know whether we were allowed to call it Indian summer anymore, but that's what it was. I could see a couple of stars overhead emerging in the twilight. The light changed considerably in the late fall, once the leaves had fallen. Our streets were canopied, heavy with leaves, all summer, and then in the fall, it was as if the ceiling had been lifted and we could see stars among the branches, could see moonlight for the first time in ages right in town.

Many of the leaves that had been bright tender buds when Arthur died now crunched under my feet and smelled of decay. I thought about how shale gas was made of organic matter that had decayed over slow millennia. We might think that what was buried was done with, that now was all that mattered—and yet, even the most ephemeral of things, these dried up leaves or the ache for a husband, never really went away.

I passed Lee Henshall's old house and there was a dumpster in the driveway and I could see that all the walls inside had been painted white. After my granddaddy died, my grandmother had hired a man to whitewash all the walls of the house. She said that was what you did. You made a blank canvas and you started again. I tried to imagine all the walls of my house cleaned of bookshelves and painted white and I couldn't imagine it. I could concede that Nick was right about the carpet, that that much of a fresh start would be a good idea, but white walls felt frightening to me, as if I would disappear as well as Arthur.

Oddly, I thought of Arthur and the salt. I had tried to cook so well for Arthur but when I found food squirreled away in his desk and in the piles of personal effects they sent home for him, afterwards—I realized it had not all been up to me. I had been furious. I had stopped salting our food—but he had bags of roasted peanuts and cashews that had perhaps sealed his fate. I would have done anything to make him well again—and now as I thought of the saltless diet I had endured, I suddenly craved salt potatoes and chicken. Maybe it was that it was autumn now or maybe it had been the earthquake, but I ached with a deep sense of loss and it was all I could do to keep from sobbing as I walked.

We do the best we can, choose cheerfulness and constancy in our circumstances, because really what is our alternative? And yet, after a certain point in life, our options, perhaps like our arteries or our vision if we are unlucky, narrow. We make our choices, have our reasons, live with our consequences. But in the end, we lose what we have, whether through disease and death, retirement or even the benign fact that our children grow up and away, depriving us of the role that gave us purpose and vitality.

And then I stopped, right on the corner of Utica and Lincoln, and I spoke out loud: "Not this one."

My mouth hung open with a kind of shock and I felt a chill at my realization. Fracking was no act of God, no freak of nature. Left the way things were naturally, we could continue to drink lakewater, grow apples, press them into cider and raise a glass. Fracking was no colony collapse of uncertain origin. The decay it caused was in no way inevitable.

Except, unless.

Except if we simply let them in to frack our land. Unless we failed to stand in the way. If we watched and let them when it didn't look like a good idea. If we trusted big business to do what was best for the land and lakes and community we loved, that would be a kind of colony collapse.

It was not too late for this one.

This one was up to me, or at least was one where I could make a difference. I thought of Carmel and her father—are you a fracktivist, he had asked. Perhaps this was how you became one. What I knew was that I felt steadied. I could hear a train in the distance, but the only other sound was the flapping of wings as Canada geese flew overhead. It was a sound as quiet as a heartbeat, a steady pumping, carrying them away.

I woke up the next morning with a sense of purpose. I put away the dishes from the previous night, and drank most of a pot of coffee, waiting until the bookstore opened.

I was brimming with energy and so I walked downtown to the Commons and to the bookstore. My walk was very different from the night before—I knew now that this issue mattered. I had heard Carmel talk about her trees drinking water from down deep. As I waded through leaves and looked at the sturdy trunks that stood sentinel on my street, I thought suddenly of the verse as Jesus went into Jerusalem where he said, "if these are quiet, even the stones will cry out." It made me think of the trip across the southwest where Arthur drove and I read the entire Lord of the Rings trilogy to Nick to keep him occupied. I thought of the Ents opposing the orcs and the building of Mordor and the works of evil—and I wondered how these trees would cry out if we were silent.

I felt like I saw everything around me with compassionate eyes, responsible eyes. It reminded me of watching Nick and his friends at their graduation, the sense of ownership I felt for boys who were not my own, the sense that they too were mine to protect and defend and love. That was how I felt for the mountains that rose around me, the trees that stood tall and firm, the students I passed, the mothers and babies.

I walked up the staircase again and through the little café, and the office at the front was unlocked. The room was littered with desks and posters and room dividers: You want to be an activist? Pick your cause here. There was a wide variety of causes spread throughout the room, but surprisingly no people. I walked around and saw the various concerns. It was a bit like a craft sale or a science fair, with each group pushing their own agenda.

At the anti-fracking desk, there was a clipboard where you could sign up for their email newsletter and another for the blockade road trip. There was a poster about an anti-fracking zombie movie being made that was looking for extras. I picked up the first clipboard and started to fill in my contact information. And then they asked for my skills and passions. I sighed: cooking soup, I thought, and raising my son. Those were the main things I had to offer. I left that blank and instead signed my name and email address on the Pennsylvania bus trip list. I had to laugh: I had resisted the shopping bus trips and the Mennonite bus trips to Pennsylvania with the seniors from church, and now here I was.

I walked out of the office and down the stairs, feeling my heart thump in my chest, my eyes as bright and dazzled as if I had a fever. At the bottom of the steps, I saw Henry standing there, his head turned sideways, looking at book titles. I could have squeezed past him, likely without him seeing me, but I needed someone to share this moment with me.

"Henry." I grabbed his arm. "You'll never guess what I've just done."

He looked up and smiled. "What have you done?"

"I've signed up to be part of a blockade."

He shifted a stack of books on his hip. "What do you mean?"

"Did you feel the earthquake yesterday? I'm going to go with a busload of people to Pennsylvania. To protest."

He shook his head. "Wait a minute. This sounds like a longer story. Do you have time for a coffee?"

Coffee was exactly what I didn't need. I could use a glass

of wine or a drink of cool water, but I followed him to the counter where he paid for his books and then we stepped outside. He held my arm at the elbow, gently guiding me along. I felt like I needed it, like I could go off in a million directions, like I could explode with excitement. His hand felt like dancing, like someone was leading me.

He led me into the café that I called the hobbit restaurant. It was covered in wood and macramé and hanging plants. Henry paid for two coffees and I found a chair at a table made of a slice of tree. It seemed like a good place for an activist. A fracktivist. I said the word under my breath while I waited for him to come to the table.

"So," he said, handing me a mug.

"So," I said and I could feel my heartbeat in my fingertips against the handle. "So, in my old age, I've decided to become a protester. I'm going to go with some of my classmates to Pennsylvania to protest a fracking well."

"Hold on a minute. Classmates? Fracking well?"

"You remember the signs, the fracking signs?" And then I realized he had fed me honey when I was sick but he had no idea of this class, this idea that had invaded my life like a virus. I took a sip of coffee. "I decided to take a course with Ben to find out more about fracking."

"And what exactly is this fracking anyhow?"

I had spent more than a month on this and I should be able to explain it. "You know how this whole area is covered with shale? Apparently when it was formed, 400 million years ago, it trapped bits of material that have turned into little bubbles of natural gas, deep in the earth.

"In order to get it out, the frackers dig a well and blast water, sand and chemicals into the earth, fracturing the shale and releasing the gas. They suck it back up the well and separate out the gas from the water. Or they try to. The problem is how little they can actually retrieve and the chemicals they leave behind at the surface and in the water table. Also fracking isn't exactly good for stability—shale is brittle."

"Hence the earthquake yesterday?" He looked skeptical.

"It could be. They're fracking in Pennsylvania. Anyhow, it was enough to convince me to go protest."

"But, if it's that bad, why would they even consider it?"

"Because they can frack enough to fuel the whole US for years. And fracking provides jobs. And the companies offer tantalizingly large amounts of money for the drilling rights. If you own a farm and aren't sure whether you can make the mortgage payments and pay for fertilizer, it starts to look pretty attractive, those offers."

Carmel hadn't said whether Amos had accepted the offer or not and I had seen his bearded face in class for a couple of weeks but I had been afraid to ask.

"Electrical grids won't run themselves," he said.

"I know. But it doesn't make it right—just because we need something."

"I hear you." He looked at his watch and then downed the rest of his coffee. "I told Jane I was just going to pick up a couple of books. I should get going. I'm happy for you,

though, Daisy. It sounds like something worth fighting for."
He stood up and then leaned over to say something quietly
and I turned to hear it. But he wasn't trying to say something.
Instead his lips landed on my earlobe, soft and unexpected. I
had expected sound and instead was touched.

"I thought you were trying to say something," I said.

I had turned handfuls of Carmel's misshapen apples into
the sweetest of soups—apple-cheddar-onion—the night she
arrived with Aurora in hand.

"It is Wednesday nights, right?" she said. "Your dinner?"

"Of course. Come in," I said. "No, don't worry about your
shoes."

Some of the Asian students were fascinated by Aurora's
white-blonde hair and they touched it. Carmel had
still not found a home for her puppy and so I made an
announcement, and then Ben muttered something and
everyone around him laughed.

I found Carmel in the kitchen at the end of the night,
talking with Cecily about the restaurant, and washing dishes.
I no longer turned away offers of dishwashing help.

"You should try it," Cecily was saying.

"Try what?" I asked, and then bit my tongue: my mother
had taught me better than that.

"She's thinking about making a little café on her farm."

"Not a café. That's too much. I just thought maybe if we set up a couple of tables and served apple pie and maybe a soup like this, and coffee."

"Oh," I said. "A café."

Cecily laughed. "Exactly."

"In your garage where you keep the apples?" I said.

She nodded. "There or just out front."

I nodded. "I think it would be a great fit. Can you see the lake from there?"

"If you know where to look."

"So, you're in the fracking course with Daisy?" Cecily asked. "Are you surviving that jerk?"

"Ben?" I said.

"You want to see the best in everyone, Daisy, but trust me, I know jerk."

Cecily had found a lump and lost a husband in the same year. Cecily's husband had lost his mother to cancer, and Cecily never knew whether he was scared it was contagious or whether he was simply unable to rise to the challenge, but he had left and moved in with a woman whose breasts were more than intact, who rippled with massive silicone implants. The contrast and the irony were not lost on Cecily.

She walked out to the dining room to get more dishes and Carmel picked up the jar of honey from the counter and wiped it off. She looked over at me, her eyes blue and bright.

"He likes you," she said. "You know that, right?"

I frowned. "Ben?"

She gestured with the honey. Henry.

Cecily came back into the room and said Aurora was falling

asleep in front of the television. Carmel looked at her watch.

"I've got to get to the hardware store before it closes," she said. "And before she loses it. I'm sorry to leave you with all the dishes, Daisy Jane."

I followed her into the hallway where she found her coat on the pegs, and wrapped Aurora in hers. I wanted to finish the conversation. He's married, I wanted to say. He's a friend. I've told him he doesn't need to bring honey but he says bees make more honey than they can eat, that in a warm fall they will fill the brood area with honey if he doesn't harvest it.

"I signed up," I said to her instead. "I signed up for that road trip to Pennsylvania." Her eyes grew wide and she threw her arm around me in a one-armed hug. "I'll see you at class tomorrow." As I stood in the doorway and watched her buckle the baby into the truck and climb in the other side, I could smell the patchouli scent that, of course, was Carmel, and then she honked the horn briefly and drove off.

My not mentioning what she had said about Henry said I had already forgotten it, that it was insignificant, inconsequential, a small fragment in a multi-layered life.

When I was a little girl, I had a bicycle that had been my older brother's. I learned to ride it almost without being taught and I rode it everywhere I could. There was one big hill in our town and my brother rode down it hands-free and up it halfway, hands-free. I had watched him race cars down that hill on his bike, narrowly staying on the pavement and not straying into the gravel. It did not look hard to do. One day, I rode my bike to the top of the hill and set forth downhill. What I did not know about was how gravity worked, how speed increased as I went. I was halfway down the hill, panic-stricken. I went over my handlebars in a succession of somersaults and scrapes a dozen times in my mind. It was terrifying. By the time I reached the bottom of the hill, my hands were cramped in a death-grip on the handlebars so that I could not let go, even as I covered my brother's bicycle with vomit.

This was the picture that came to my mind as I leaned over the toilet bowl in the middle of the night. I had awoken with a feeling that I was careening downhill with no brakes on a bicycle that would soon flip me over and render me entirely broken. I raced to the restroom and emptied my dinner into the toilet. And then I sat on the floor as I had not done in years, and I shook for an hour, until every muscle in my body ached and I knew I had to make myself stop.

Above the fridge was where we kept Arthur's whisky. For Arthur, whisky was a man's drink after supper on an autumn evening. It was the smell of woodsmoke on a cold night. I had never liked it, but I craved something for purely medicinal purposes, something that would stun my system into quiet once again. I found a stool and uncapped the whisky and poured some into a coffee mug. And then I sat at the kitchen table taking little sips of it until my head turned fuzzy and my mind cleared and the sun started to come up.

I had heard of white nights before, but I had never been prone to them. At the edge of my mind as I sat staring into the darkness, I kept trying to look for the reason why—the earthquake? the road trip? the kiss?—but I knew that night-thoughts were scarcely more coherent than dreams. I also felt that if I examined the thoughts too closely in the dark of night, I might actually drown.

I went back to bed when I could and slept for a couple of hours. When I woke, I was myself again, but I felt dislocated and aching all over, as if I had been in a car accident. I was hungry—it had not been flu or something I had eaten—but I did not know what I wanted.

And then I did. I wanted my mother to spoon soft pudding into my mouth, the way she had when I was a child and was sick. Soft pudding might very well have been bread soaked in milk, with a splash of maple syrup and an egg. It was not so much the ingredients or the taste as the spooning. I wanted to be small and cosseted and petted, to be little Daisy again.

I knew what I didn't want: to get the winter tires put on the car. And yet, that's what I had to do. I got up and I found I was still shaky. This was one of Arthur's jobs. I had looked all week for the tires and they had squeezed me in at the garage. But I felt I couldn't go.

I wondered whether I would have to make myself go, whether there was anyone else I could call. Cecily was at work. I was tempted to call Henry, but I thought back to Peg Parsons' reaction to Bill's offer to clean my eavestroughs: was it right to borrow another woman's husband? I decided I would call but I would hang up if Jane answered the phone. I decided I wouldn't think too much about that decision either.

But it was Henry who picked up the phone.

"I had an upset stomach in the night," I said, feeling that only those facts were certain. "I was wondering whether you might be free to take my car in for an oil change and to get the winter tires on it." For a brief moment I thought about the idea of asking him to feed me and I had to bite the inside of my cheek to keep from bursting into hysterical laughter that would have frightened him more than if I vomited at his feet. "At ten. They told me that they always kept the tires there for us. They have an attic above the shop where they keep the tires and they label each person's tires." I stopped. Henry did not need to know the geography of our mechanic's garage.

"Ten o'clock?" he said.

"Yes."

"I'd be happy to help you."

"I'll leave the keys on the table inside the door. I think I'm going to head back to sleep."

"I'll find them," he said, kindly. "You go back to bed."

"Thank you." I said.

I woke up again around noon. I felt hungry, which I thought was a good sign. I went downstairs and saw my keys still on the table, but beside them was a takeout cup, a packet of sugar, a creamer and a note.

"Hope you're feeling better," the note said. "I thought you might like a cup of tea. I wasn't sure whether you took milk or sugar so I got them both. H."

Tea was in the soft pudding family, a cousin a few steps removed, but still the kind of thing that made it possible for chasms to be breached and worlds to be righted after a tempest. "Thank you." I said out loud. "Tea is just what I need."

Carmel was wrong: Henry was a good man and a good friend.

But it was Nick I wanted too, wanted like a hen settling a chick under her wing. The earthquake and the white night told me that. I wanted to be able to know that Nick was safe. Nick worked on the 114th floor of his office building. High enough that he could feel the building sway in a storm. High enough that, if it were the Twin Towers, he would be above the impact, stuck, lost.

It was after the earthquake in Indonesia that I had started going back to church. The nice thing about the Catholic church is that people just expect you to go. There is no prodigal-returning celebration. You're just folded back in. It was the Women's Auxiliary that made the tunafish sandwiches the week of Arthur's funeral, and I was grateful for that, even if I couldn't eat any. There was my Sunday School class—old enough to read and reason but too young for irony and eyeliner. There was the annual bazaar. On Sunday, there had been a note about the upcoming bazaar in the bulletin. Part craft sale, part rummage sale and part bake sale, people brought what they could, and we generally came home with more than we brought. For years, I had contributed jars of pickles and green tomato relish, but this time when I saw the notice in the church bulletin, it made me think again about cleaning out my house, that I could bring things to the bazaar. I had not finished cleaning out Arthur's study: once the class had started, it felt like my week filled up more than I had expected. Being sick had not helped either. I had circled the bazaar in the bulletin and stuck it into my purse, but when I got home, I could only walk around my house. It was too much, too soon to think of cleaning out my house for the bazaar.

I settled on the couch with the warm tea that would protect me and I thought about the road trip to Pennsylvania. Carmel had said it was unrealistic to think someone could go from actively supporting fracking to actively opposing it, that it was a matter of small shifts, shifting people from neutral to passive allies, and then passive allies to active allies. I wondered as I felt the aches from the night before whether I had tried to take too many steps in this too. In any event, I didn't think I could do it. I wasn't a protester. But I didn't want to see Carmel's face when I told her at class that night either.

7
White Bean & Tarragon Soup

Some people had been raised to never show up without
a hostess gift. I had received countless bottles of wine on
Wednesdays over the years, but also less conventional gifts:
vats of kimchi and sauerkraut, bouquets of radishes, soap and
rubber gloves, small figurines, books and candy. The fact that
Henry brought honey was no more remarkable than the fact
that Cecily brought bread or that I made soup. It was what we
did.

But on the following Wednesday night, Henry came with
a honey jar filled with roses, ivory and pinks and peach, all
wide open and almost overblown, trailing petals behind him
like a fairy tale up my porch steps. He held them out to me
and I shook my head, a fluttering in my stomach and the
sweet scent rising in the air.

"They're from Jane," he said. "It's the last of the roses and
she said I should bring them and let them be enjoyed."

I leaned forward to smell the roses and the petals brushed
against my skin, soft as a cheek themselves, and the smell was
intoxicating.

"They won't last long but I thought you'd like them."

His explanation was utterly reasonable in every way: Jane
could not enjoy the roses and so he had brought them as a

nice last hurrah of fall to adorn the community table. It was fine, it was acceptable to take the flowers, to say thank you, to place them on the table, to tell everyone that Jane had sent them, to make a container of soup to send home with Henry with our thanks. Our thanks, I wrote on the lid and I signed it The Wednesday Night Crew. It didn't explain why my hands shook as I wrote.

It also didn't explain why I didn't recognize Lee Henshall when she showed up in my kitchen half an hour later. Father Jim jokingly called my Wednesday suppers my 'widows and orphans' meal. I suppose he was right, to some extent, but aside from Nick's friend Jamie who lived with us for a year after his parents split up, I had never seen someone so needy before.

To be fair, Lee had retired from the university more than a year before, had sold her house and moved away. Then too, she was jetlagged, and that was part of it. But she looked uncertain, which was likely why I didn't recognize her at first. Lee had always been certain of herself—tall, confident, independent. To be honest, she had always reminded me of a man. When Arthur had first told me Lee Henshall was coming to supper, that Lee was a professor in the English department, I had expected a man.

Cornell was founded on co-educational principles, as they always reminded us at convocations each year, women had always been valued as much as men had, but I still wondered what the cost had been to women like Lee, who had taught before it was common for women to be called doctor.

And now, she didn't look like a man—or a woman, in fact. She looked like a stray kitten that needed feeding and was afraid to come in out of the rain. And it had been raining, cold and heavy, October rain. We had been to her farewell dinner and even to the auction at her house, when she got rid of a number of her belongings. And now here she was, lurking in the doorway, shrinking her height as low as she could. I had always been slightly intimidated by Lee, jealous of the way she could keep up with Arthur intellectually, but I didn't feel that way when I saw her in the shadows of my kitchen.

She reached into her pocket, as you might reach for a weapon if you were a woman walking the streets alone at night. Which I suppose she was.

I was cutting the bread that Cecily had brought from the restaurant, end-of-day bread, listening to Cecily's stories about the customers who couldn't understand the lack of meat on the menu, when I looked up and saw Lee.

She handed me a package, shrink-wrapped plastic, and it was cheese. "Straight from Italy," she said, and she sounded like Lee.

"Thank you," I said. "I didn't know you were back in town. Are you visiting?"

She shook her head. "I'm hoping to stay." She said it quickly.

"Welcome back," I said, handing her a bowl. "Should I cut your cheese up?"

"If you want," she said.

The cheese was fragrant and crumbled under my knife. I

cut a little and ate it myself.

Lee sat on a stool in the kitchen and sipped her soup in silence.

I got busy in the living room with some international students who were trying to explain bus routes to one another. And then I had to stop a toddler from playing with my china horse collection. I remembered I hadn't made coffee and when I came out to the kitchen, Lee was still sitting on the stool, her eyes not quite focused.

"More soup?" I asked.

"No thanks," she said.

"The cheese is delicious," I said. "So you've been to Italy?"

"For the summer," she said. "I just got back yesterday."

"I've never been to Italy," I said, measuring the coffee. "I've heard it's lovely."

"It really was," she agreed. I poured water into the pot and turned it on. Henry came into the kitchen with his honey, brown as maple.

"I forgot to give this to you earlier," he said. It felt like surfeit.

"Thank you," I said. "Did you see who's back in town?"

"Lee Henshall," he said. "I thought you'd moved to Arizona."

"I missed the weather here," she said, drily, and he laughed.

"But, really, you're back?"

She nodded and I watched her out of the corner of my eye as I wiped the counters.

"Where are you living?"

"Right now, I'm staying at the Holiday Inn," she said. "Until I get my bearings."

"She just got back yesterday," I said.

"Well, to the US yesterday. I took the bus here today."

"You'd be welcome to stay here for a while," I said. "I've got lots of room."

"Oh God," she said. "Arthur. I'm so sorry. Forgive me. I'm so tired I didn't even tell you I'm sorry about Arthur."

So she had heard.

"Thank you," I said. "It was a terrible shock."

She nodded.

"I've got plenty of room," I said, and then realized I had said that before, and I wondered if my loneliness shone out like a beacon. I was very aware that Henry stood at the side of the room, leaning on the refrigerator.

Her eyes focused then and she looked at me. I wasn't sure what she was measuring or evaluating, exactly.

"Why don't you come over for dinner," I said. "We can talk about how it might work." What I didn't want to admit to myself or her was that I felt safer with someone else in the house. It wasn't that I was afraid of burglars any more than was prudent. But I had been married just short of forty years and I had no idea how to be a single woman again.

The day with Henry at the lake had shown me that. It had not occurred to me what the neighbors might say or think— and fortunately, I suppose they're so used to people coming and going from my house, that it didn't apparently even register that Daisy was going out for a picnic with a man. It wasn't like I had come home after dark, or the following day. I hadn't stopped either to think of what could happen, alone by a lake, without neighbors. And then he had come and stood in my kitchen and had fed me honey and lemon and now he had brought me roses. I didn't think Carmel was right but I could still feel his kiss on my ear.

Lee nodded and we settled on Sunday.

The petals had fallen off half the roses by the next morning, and they lay on the dining room table like lingerie discarded in a flurry. I gathered them in my hands and they were supple and cool as flesh. I put them in the composter with the apple peelings and all the cores of my life and they shone bright and colorful as a circus against the rotting matter in the box. The petals on my stairs outside stayed stuck, a trail. I tried to take them off but it was not worth the scraping. They would come off with the snow. In the meantime, they made me remember and not forget.

It had been two years since Arthur and I had been intimate: he had been afraid after his first heart trouble and I had been just finishing up with the menopause then, finishing with a bang that made me glad to sleep on my own, to throw the covers off with no one to complain. He had always been a night owl too, coming to bed very late, disturbing my sleep. This way, we had each been able to maintain our needs.

I had taken over the guest room, leaving ours to Arthur.

The guest room was smaller—it had been Nick's when he was small. Most nights I still slept there, but some nights when I was very lonely, I climbed in our bed and slept on Arthur's side. Now, with the possibility of Lee coming, I had to pick a room for myself and one for her. There were reasons on both sides: our room had a small ensuite bathroom and I thought I would welcome the privacy, but the guest room had a sloped ceiling and Lee was as tall as a man. Still, what did it mean to cede the master bedroom to someone new? And perhaps to Lee in particular. There had been a time when I could tell that Arthur was attracted to her, attracted to her mind. A wife of a professor, though, had to let such suspicions go or they would take over.

She came with a bottle of white wine. I had made the Cornell chicken and salt potatoes I'd been craving, and a salad. We weren't exactly friends. It felt like we were playing it safe.

"I've never had anything but soup here," she said, with a nervous laugh as I brought the chicken out.

I wasn't sure how she would feel about me saying grace. It was like that.

"I thought we should talk about this a bit more," I said. "To figure out how this might work."

"I'm happy to pay you," she said.

"I was thinking more about what we both wanted."

She nodded and took a swallow of wine. And as much as she looked like a stray, I couldn't think of a specific topic to ask her about.

"Can I ask you," I said, "what made you come back to Ithaca?"

"Sure," she said. "Well, I spent last winter in Arizona with my sister, and my brain dried out from all the shopping and tennis. So, in March, I escaped to Florida as I always had on my sabbaticals, but when spring training came to an end and it got hotter, I didn't know what to do with myself. I went on the Internet every day and looked at the weather in Ithaca, read the news in the paper. That's where I read that Arthur had died."

"I wondered who had told you," I said.

"I signed up for a course so my mind wouldn't collapse altogether. It was Italian because I had thought I might spend the summer in Italy. When I went to Italy, it was hotter than Florida even, and the only Italian words I needed were *glace* and *gelata* —ice and ice cream.

"I made the rounds and went to Pompeii, more because it was there than anything else, but I found myself going back to the ruins day after day. There was a girl there, painfully thin, with a sketchbook. It makes you want to live, doesn't it? she said. We sat in the shade on a bench together and I passed her slices of blood orange I'm not sure she ate.

"One day, she asked me where I was from and I said Ithaca and suddenly I knew that was true. I read somewhere once that baseball is the only sport where the goal was to head home, and that was the moment I decided to come back."

I had finished my chicken by then. I remembered something Arthur had once said, that people in Ithaca cared more about the provenance of their food—Arthur used to joke that one day soon he'd hear people asking the name of the pig they were eating—and less about where people came from. Many places, it mattered, you mattered more if you'd been born and bred there. Here you could be grafted in. Many of us were. And eventually it became home.

"Can I warm your supper up?" I asked.

"Is that a way of saying I'm long winded?"

I hoped it was a joke.

She laughed. "It's fine. So, that's how I got back here. It's a little embarrassing really to be at loose ends."

"I know what that's like," I said.

She nodded. "How long has it been now?"

"Six and a half months," I said. More than half a year since I'd been at the dentist and the receptionist interrupted my cleaning, her face ashen. They had found me because my appointment was listed in Arthur's day planner. The receptionist had driven me to the hospital but he had died instantly and there was nothing I could do but feel the contrast between the teeth that had been polished and those that were still encrusted with tartar. My tongue played around in my mouth with those teeth while my mind reeled and my stomach churned. It was like a rosary. The leaves had come out on the trees the week of the funeral. And every day in front of the one before, a fog, a mist, a slight clearing, an occasional downpour. Now it had cleared and the landscape was the same but at the same time very different.

"I'm taking a course at the university," I said, passing her the salad bowl again.

She looked at me with a startled people-still-go-to-college look.

"A geology course."

"Geology," she said, looking amused.

"Yes, geology," I said, wondering for the first time if I could live with this woman. She had put her fork and knife at an angle on her plate. "Would you like to see around upstairs?" I asked.

"Sure."

She followed me up the stairs. "This was Arthur's and my room," I said. "But it's going to be yours."

"I'm not kicking you out of your room."

"I've been sleeping in the spare room the last six months." Liar, I thought. "The ceiling would be too low for you in the spare room, and this way, you can have your own restroom."

She walked into the room and through to the restroom. "No shower?" she said.

"Just a tub," I said. "There's a shower in the basement."

"Is there a room in the basement?" she asked.

I nodded. Nick had lived in the basement through his high school years. I led her down the stairs. Other than the bend in the stairs where the ceiling was low due to ducts, she didn't have to stoop at all. Arthur had forgotten to accommodate that bend every single time he walked down the stairs, and hit his head regularly. It had been one of the few things, besides Christmas tree stands, that made him curse.

"Laundry room," I said, giving the tour. "Bar, restroom,

workshop, Nick's room." Nick had cleaned everything he needed out of the room years before, and all that was left was a chrysalis of his high school self. I hadn't been able to bring myself to take down the Nirvana and Jamaican Olympic bobsled team posters or to remove the weights he had lifted every day, even though I stored my out-of-season clothes in his closet.

Lee was smiling. "Weirdly," she said, "I think it's me."

Weirdly, I thought she might be right. There was a lot I thought we should talk about: should we cook together, how will we arrange parking, how will we divide chores, quiet hours, Wednesday nights, pets, my need for quiet, toilet roll over or under, how long will you be staying, but I decided it could wait. We could work it out along the way.

Lee looked around the room. "Thank you for doing this, Daisy," she said. "It's really...brave of you." I was surprised by her word. I had expected her to say it was kind. "I'll try to be decent. And I won't forget it's your house."

I nodded.

"I've paid at the Holiday Inn until the end of the month. I could move in on the first."

"Sure."

"I don't know how long I'll be here for."

"Let's see how it goes," I said. "Did you want dessert?"

"Actually, what I want is to see the score in the game."

"The game?"

"Oh God, Daisy, it's Game 6 of the American League championship."

The candy had started to appear in the stores in early September but I hadn't given it more than a moment's thought until the day after supper with Lee. Halloween had always and forever been Arthur's domain. He wasn't one for the macabre, but he dressed up every year and sat in a chair on our front porch. He believed in the literal truth of trick or treat and because he gave out full-sized candy bars, the kids in our neighborhood planned ahead for Halloween. They came with magic tricks and skipping ropes, with whoopee cushions and fake hooks. Those who did left with smiles and chocolate enough to rot their teeth.

I found myself in the drug store the day before Halloween, stocking up on more Kleenex, when I noticed the Halloween candy display had dwindled alarmingly. I had given no real thought to what I would do, had not reevaluated the tradition. I wasn't about to dress up, but neither would I shut out the lights and pretend the streets were not filled with roaming, excited children.

I had loved those years, the years of walking around with Nick, until he grew old enough that he wanted to go out with his friends, and then too old to go out at all. I loved the fact that there was a night a year that people opened their doors to children and to one another. It was usually cold and rainy by the end of October, and sometimes there was even snow, and Halloween was like a taste of summer all over again, a chance to catch up with people who had gotten busy with life. I suppose that was what Wednesday nights had become too, but Halloween was that, for children. I had always been surprised by the people who thought it was wrong; to me, it was very right. And to Arthur, it was a kind of sacred ritual, in a man not often known for whimsy. I had loved that about him.

Arthur had worn a variety of different masks over the years—and I got them out and placed one or two on the table by the door where I had the chocolate bars. The masks were rubber and they frightened me now, deflated, eyeless faces on a table. Fear was now a familiar feeling to me. My stomach was already tight. I put the masks away before supper, a meal I could not eat. I kept seeing the masks in my mind, masks that had been filled with Arthur, masks that were as lifeless as his face now was.

It did not help when the first child rang the doorbell and asked where Mr. Scarecrow was. I had not prepared a response that was adequate to a costumed child. I was not adequate to the situation.

"He's not here," was all I said. And then to forestall more questions. "He told me that there would be kids coming with tricks for me."

The boy held out his hand and I reached out and shook it— and got an electrical shock. The boy guffawed and I held back tears. It had not hurt so much as surprised me. I blinked back tears as I turned to the silver tray on which, as usual, I had laid out a variety of full-sized chocolate bars.

"Well, you tricked me," I said, wearing my own kind of mask as I held the tray out to him.

Should Halloween—All Hallow's Eve—be a time to talk of death, to remember death, to remember the ones who had passed on? The next day was All Saints Day and I knew my church would hold a service for the dead. It suddenly all seemed as macabre as it was originally meant to be, only the masks brought death closer, rather than scaring it away. It was genuinely all I could do not to turn out the lights and retreat to my bed. I had time to sit and wait between children, but I could not come up with a good way of addressing Arthur's absence. I wished Lee had already moved in. By the fourth or fifth time I answered the door, just as the light in the sky was fading altogether, I decided that I could not answer the question at all. I threw the door open at the muffled call of trick or treat and put a hand on my hip and smiled broadly,

"Give me a trick," I said and I was in the costume of a confident, happy woman. One who was pulling off a trick with great success as no one asked me again about Arthur. It was the trick they wanted most of all, the chance to perform and be admired and plied with chocolate. And what I could not, would not, let myself think about was the kinds of magic tricks where a magician could make someone disappear and reappear. I looked out at the little bench in front of the house, the bench from which Arthur would call for me to bring the tray with chocolate bars for the young magicians, and wished that he would suddenly materialize there, in costume or not.

I could almost hear his voice and I certainly could hear it in my head, which might have been a conjuring trick in itself because I had not been able to call up his face or his voice for weeks.

It was almost the end of the night when a pickup truck pulled up in front of my house. I watched between the heads of two high school boys in hockey gear, who were collecting cans for the food bank, and saw that it was Carmel and her toddler, dressed as a dog.

"Daisy Jane!" Carmel called, hoisting the child onto her hip.

I had just handed the boys the last of the candy.

"Come in," I said. "I'm all cleaned out but you can come in."

"It's not like she needs candy," Carmel said, climbing the steps. "I just thought you'd like to see my other puppy."

Aurora stuck her tongue out and licked her mother's cheek.

"Do you want something to drink?" I asked.

Carmel laughed. "I would—but I've got miles to go before I sleep. Actually, I'd love a glass of water."

She put Aurora down and followed me into the kitchen. I put the kettle on and looked at my supper, cold on the table. I covered it and was about to put it in the fridge.

"Did you get supper?" I asked her.

"Well, no," she said. "But we're fine."

"I have lots of food. I'm still working on this cooking for one person." I thought of Lee who was moving in the next day and wondered whether she would let me cook for her.

Aurora walked into the kitchen, wearing a Ronald Reagan mask that was probably as old as her mother. I burst into nearly hysterical laughter and leaned against the counter as she bumped into Carmel's leg, only one eye able to look out of the sockets.

I had made a small bowl of pasta but it wouldn't stretch to two so I found the leftover soup—white bean and tarragon—from Wednesday night and poured it into a saucepan. Carmel hadn't been back since the time she had visited so she didn't have to know it was left over.

"Has Aurora eaten?" I asked.

"I gave her some Cheerios and tofu before we left and she's probably jacked up on sugar now, so I have no idea whether she's hungry or not. She can have some of mine."

"I haven't eaten either," I said. "Do you mind if I join you?"

"Of course not," Carmel said. "Can I wash up?"

"Go ahead," I said. "The restroom is just down the hall on your—"

"I'm fine here," Carmel said and she turned the kitchen faucet on. When her own hands were clean, she picked up Aurora, minus the Reagan face, but still in her fuzzy dog costume and washed her hands and face at the sink. I remembered that hip-hold, holding a child up and freeing my hands to help, while using my hip to pin him at the sink. I ladled soup into bowls and watched hungrily.

Aurora came back with a shining wet face.

"We were at my friend's house most of the evening, making flyers and press releases about the rally."

I stopped, mid-twirl of pasta. "Rally?"

"You were at class last week, weren't you?"

I still felt cowardly about backing out of the road trip.

"The hearing that will regulate natural gas drilling in our region is on November 19 so we're having a citizen's rally against fracking that day on the Commons."

I looked at the face of Dutch on the floor, looking up at me. Arthur had worn his face as a joke—we had always been Democrats—but I had sort of liked Reagan in a non-political way. I had liked that he was willing to take on politics at his age, that he was able to cut through complicated jargon and rhetoric with simplicity. I always remembered something Reagan had said once, "Don't be afraid to see what you see."

What I saw was a scared Daisy. My life had been small but now it was too small. I had never protested because there had never been something I had wanted to protest. And now I did but I was scared.

"How was Pennsylvania?" I asked.

She rolled her eyes. "You didn't miss much. It was wet and they drove around us in their big trucks and no media came."

"I'm sorry."

"You win some, you lose some. We didn't get arrested."

"Do you want more soup?"

"No, but it was delicious." I carried our bowls to the sink. When I turned, she was looking thoughtfully at the Reagan mask. "Well, it was three years ago tonight that Aurora was conceived. Trick or treat, huh?"

I nodded slowly, not sure what to say. The child settled back in her mother's lap, her head drooping while Carmel looked out the window, almost as if she had forgotten I was there, her face slack and younger looking than it usually was. I wondered how old she actually was.

"We had harvested early." She shifted slightly in her chair and her eyes drifted as she spoke. "And we hired a couple of university students, friends of my brother's, to help us out.

"It was probably the most fun I'd had at a bottling party since my grandfather let me stay up all night when I was 12. And most of it was because of this one guy. He was a med student and he was tall and beautiful and I could see his muscles ripple under his shirt while he was lifting cases of bottles in and out of the sterilizer and the canner.

"We always drink the dregs of the cider that's left over. I still don't know if it was the cider or the pheromones after weeks of being covered with apple pulp and sweat.

"Around four in the morning, I went outside to get something from the shed—corks, I think it was, for the bottler, and I looked up and at first, I thought that what I saw was streaks of dawn in the sky, and then I realized it was the Northern Lights. I had never seen them before—have you ever seen them, Daisy Jane?"

I shook my head.

"It was almost eerie. I ran inside to tell the guys, but only Jake was there just then. He came out with me to see and we ended up sitting in the back of my truck, watching the pillars of light dancing in the sky for probably fifteen minutes before he kissed my neck and that was that."

I found myself touching my earlobe as she spoke.

"They say a child conceived under the Northern Lights

will have a long and happy life. I know what you're thinking. Totally hippy dippy, right? Getting knocked up in the back of a truck that smelled like fermented apples under the Northern Lights."

I smiled.

"When I told Jake I was pregnant, he just wanted it gone and done with. He was scared. I see that now. But I was scared too and hormonal. I didn't want anything from him. I just wanted that night to be preserved. And I guess it was— preserved in the form of this little imp.

"He was a good biological father for her, but an asswipe of a person."

"Does he have any contact with her—with you—at all?" I asked.

Her eyes focused and rolled at me, as if I were crazy. "We're in firm agreement on that. I make no claims on him and he can forget that he has a child. He's out of state now, anyhow, my brother says, doing his residency somewhere out west."

"I'm sorry."

She shrugged. "It was the best night of my life, Aurora's the best thing that ever happened to me and I don't have to see him anymore."

"You're brave."

"I'm a farmer, Daisy Jane. I save my anger for what really matters."

"You're just a baby yourself," I said. "How did you learn to be so wise?"

She slid the sleeping toddler onto the bench beside her and

shook out her cramped shoulders. "Thanks for saying it," she said, smiling. "I could say the trees taught me. My dad farmed for a few years, but he hated it. My grandfather loved the land, loved his trees. He taught me everything I knew. I think he knew I would take over one day—although I never got a chance to tell him. My dad insisted I go to school and get a degree—even if it was an arts degree—and I probably would have kept going if it wasn't for Aurora. So, she saved me too, from becoming what I wasn't."

"You're back in school now," I said.

"Just the one course. And it's a course my grandfather would make me take if he knew what was going on and my trees too if they could talk."

I washed the dishes after she left and thought about that until the bubbles popped and settled in the sink and the water was cool and transparent.

8
Hot and Sour Soup

Wednesday night was easier with Lee there. It was like having a husband around, but one who was a woman and who saw what needed to be done. The Wednesday after Lee came, I found myself sitting on a sofa in conversation for a good half-hour with one person or another as Lee refilled the pot of hot-and-sour soup.

She had ventured back to campus and had been given an office again as professor emeritus. She told me, as she unloaded her boxes, about her colleague who said his wife would make him attend tai chi with her if he stayed home, so he came to the office and read the newspaper for most of the day. I wasn't sure what Lee was doing. I hoped it was more than reading the newspaper.

I was passing through the living room, collecting used bowls and spoons, when I passed Lee in conversation with Henry.

"I have your Yeats," he said to her. It was an incurable habit of mine, eavesdropping. Mother's voice would forever be in my ears but I had to know who Lee's Yeats was.

"I hope you're being kind to him," she replied. It was a pet then. I pretended to adjust dried flowers in a vase in the hall around the corner from them.

"Of course. I love poetry."

I heard Lee chuckle.

"I like sonnets—I know it's the last thing you'd expect of me," he said. "I had a teacher who forced us to memorize poetry. He started with the beatniks, and we liked it for the swear words. But it was when he introduced us to sonnets that I really sat up. Sonnets were so perfect—the passion contained in such a structure."

"Good for you," said Lee. She sounded as surprised as I felt. "Does Jane like poetry?"

He laughed and I couldn't tell whether the laugh was cynical or not. "Jane's favorite poem starts, 'There was a young lady from Nantucket.'"

I suppressed a smile.

"It's okay," he said. "I recite it when I run. I like the rhythm of it, the lub-dub."

"Iambic pentameter," said Lee.

"If you say so," he said. "It matches my breathing and my step."

I hoped no one would ask me why I was standing in a darkened hallway, facing the wall.

"They kind of remind me of Wednesday suppers, sonnets do."

Oh Lord, I thought. I heard Lee chuckle again.

"How so?" she asked.

"I mean, in a way it's the same thing week after week. Just an ordinary bowl of soup. But on the other hand, it's revolutionary. Who would do something like this? Only

Daisy."

I walked away, my ears burning, remembering what Mother had always said, that eavesdroppers seldom heard good of themselves. What Henry had said there at the end had been kind and flattering, but whether it was good, I was not sure. It certainly did not leave me satisfied. I went into the kitchen and found a place for the dishes I found I still carried.

One of the grad students came over to me, shyly, then to ask if I knew of an ESL program his wife could attend. I thought of Lee and wondered. Would someone who had taught English at the university level for thirty years be insulted by the thought of it? I could see the emptiness in her days, much as I could recognize early pregnancy symptoms in another woman once I had experienced them myself.

We had begun case studies in class with students giving presentations about fracking. I was struggling with my own presentation: I wasn't sure what to write about; I couldn't see myself standing in front of the class, even for ten minutes; and I had no idea how to make or work a PowerPoint. And yet, with every word of every presentation, I was increasingly convicted that this was wrong and that all I was doing was shrugging and in effect saying "I let it happen." I thought of another of Arthur's mother's clichés: "closing the barn door after the horse has bolted." Only this horse was still inside the barn and I couldn't bring myself to close it.

Right after Arthur died, I had looked for signs in everything: sermons, graffiti, bottle-cap slogans, tee-shirts, horoscopes. If two people sent me condolences citing the same verse, I took it to be a clear message for me. Now I was doing it again, only this time I was condemned instead of comforted. In church, I looked long and hard at the quilted words at the back of the church as I waited to leave and say my goodbyes to Father Jim: Advocate Give Encourage Live it said, almost poetically to the left of the door, and then Reach Serve Learn Pray on the right. I was doing pretty well on about half of those, I thought. But Advocate and Reach made me think activism. And then, the next day I was innocently walking onto the Commons when I saw Dr. King's statue, the bust of him with the silver water falling almost on top of him, and I could see the words "until justice rains down like waters" as I hurried past and again, it felt like a message for me. A Vietnam veteran sat on a cold concrete bench in the drizzle with a sign asking for change, and I wondered what kind of change he wanted.

Lord, I thought when I woke in the night with the words long slow underwater avalanche on my lips, make it stop. I'm 58 years old. I can't do this.

Because I had learned pretty early on to roll with Wednesday nights, to not blink twice when someone came to the door, I assumed it would be a simple thing to have Lee move in.

My mother would have approved of Lee, but she would have blinked and batted and swallowed hard with more than a few of our guests. I tried to make sure her visits happened outside of Wednesdays. In the early years, we had hippies. We even had one girl who came topless a couple of times. Poor shivering thing. I had to water the soup down the next week—she helped our attendance. She had long hair and it was only when she shook her head or bent over that anyone could really see anything, but she was a bit of a sideshow nevertheless. Her name was Patty, if I remember right. She was the most out-there person we ever had, I think, but I had to be prepared for professors and their wives in suits and pearls, as well as barefoot students. I had to decide whether I was okay with shoes in the house (Shoes yes, boots no. I put out knitted slippers after the first snowfall of the season.) There was more than once that the sweet smell of pot drifted in the window from my back porch. I don't think we were ever visited by the police, but we easily could have been.

Mother would have been upset by the discussions of politics—election years were always fraught—and maybe even more by the discussion of religion. For a while, we had a Buddhist monk named Justin who joined us. He was from the Midwest but he wore the robes and shaved his head—and only one woman asked me if he had cancer. It was around the time that Justin started coming out to the dinners that I switched all the soups to vegetarian ones. A few years later, I took out any peanuts. Arthur used to grumble about that—that eventually we would be serving hot water if we

accommodated every diet out there. There have been times,
frankly, when I agreed with him—when the Atkins people
ask me about what's in a soup or the gluten-free people.
I drew the line at life-threatening and moral decisions,
although I actually decided that vegetarian was the moral line
I would hold to—I wouldn't accommodate the vegans. It was
my dinner, I decided. No one paid admission and it wasn't a
restaurant. Sometimes Cecily would bring gluten-free bread
or crackers from the restaurant and it was nice to be able to
have that option, but I wasn't running a diner, as my mother
used to say.

Although I had learned how to accommodate others, I
found it was one thing to open my home once a week to
strangers and quite another to have someone underfoot,
morning and night, even though I liked her and was glad she
had moved in.

Arthur had been a night owl and I was a morning person.
We had each found our own solitude where we needed it. But
Lee was also a morning person and I discovered that, though
I was wide awake before the sun, I didn't like to talk or even
to have people around until later in the day, especially when
I had things I needed to think about. I learned that I was
settled in my ways and that to have those ways disrupted
really felt like an affront. It was humbling. I had always seen
myself as a doer, a giver, and now I felt selfish about my time
and space.

I thought of what Henry had said about bees—how people
had figured out the ideal distance between frames of honey—

far enough that the bees wouldn't build on them but close enough that they wouldn't glue it together. We needed to figure out our own bee space, Lee and I, so we wouldn't kill each other.

By the end of the first week after she had moved in, I felt like I needed to get out of my own house. I decided I would walk down by the lake, where I could look down its length and think my own thoughts.

The sky was heavy and gray, pressing down over the city, but there was a breeze at the shore. The lakewater was clear but dark indigo at the same time. In sunshine, you could see straight to the bottom, see the shale, softened by the lapping of waves. It took a drop of water tumbling over Taughannock or Ithaca Falls at least twelve years to exit at the north end of the lake where it would travel through the end of Lake Ontario to the St. Lawrence and on to the ocean. I loved the distinctive smell of lakewater, at once fresh and stagnant. It was a simple, elemental, comforting smell—like rain or the closet of someone you loved. By summer's end, the lake was warm enough for swimming, the surface of the water warmed in the sunshine, while beneath, still cold, currents moved like rock strata. Now the surface had cooled too, chilled by the winds.

The willows at the water's edge looked ragged and tired, their leaves plastered to the ground, mixed with goose droppings and trash that had blown to the lake's shore. If I looked out at the water I could breathe deeply, but if I looked down at my feet I itched to rake and sweep and clean. But, if I was honest, I had come here as much to get away from that as anything else.

I had seen my house differently, evaluated by Lee's sharp eyes, Lee who came bearing so little and me with my collections and Arthur's things. I had moved a few things before Lee moved in. There were boxes of books I had stored in Nick's room for the last couple of years and some off-season clothes. I had stacked Nick's and my belongings behind the bar in the basement before Lee moved in, giving her space for her own belongings, but our house felt cluttered for the first time. I wondered if it was Lee's arrival or whether it was the sheer physical act of moving things around that made me see the need for change. On one hand, I knew she had just been through this a year before, auctioning off her belongings, sorting through what she would keep and what she would let go. On the other hand, I suspected she had always traveled light, whereas, I now realized, I had not. Neither had Arthur.

Part of the problem was that we had lived there so long, through years of birthdays and Christmases, Wednesday nights and daily life. And all the things that came with these years found their place, settling around us, useful or beautiful, or so I hoped. I wasn't so much a packrat, I told myself as I walked along the boardwalk, as a woman with a history, a husband and a child.

But now I was seeing things differently—that afternoon I had dusted the china horses that sat on the square panes of our bay window, the ones Mother had given me every year from the time I was nine and begged for a horse. I had been all of sixteen when I finally rode a horse for the first and last time of my life: reality had not measured up to fantasy. I wondered as I dusted each one why I had kept these, why I had them in my window. Anyone would think I was still a horse lover. I took all the horses out of the window, ostensibly to clean the window and the horses, but I had done that before many times. This time, I looked back at the window and thought about not replacing them. And then the window looked too bare, too naked, and I felt frightened.

I had put a palomino back, caressing the curve of its hind leg, and I remembered how Nick had played with the horses, so carefully. I missed that gentle cowboy.

My counters might be cluttered, my stairs stacked with books, my basement with boxes, but everything had a story to tell and without them, who would I be?

Nearly all the leaves were down, only stubborn ones remaining, but they still skidded back and forth across the path. I walked out onto the small boat landing and the impact of the wind hit me full force in the face, as it might on the bow of a boat. I needed to have my breath taken away, to be swept clean. Most of the geese and ducks were gone now for the winter, but there were still hardy seagulls, flying straight into the wind, letting the wind buffet them about. I envied them.

I decided to keep walking but then, as I regained the path, I was pretty sure I recognized a familiar figure far ahead walking toward me. I had had scares where I had thought I had seen Arthur only to have it be someone else, of course, but this one was more likely. I turned around and started to walk back toward the park entrance and home.

A minute later, from behind me I heard, "Daisy?"

I turned. "Henry," I said, demure as could be.

"I'm heading up to the lake today," he said. "My lake. You free to join me?"

"Sorry," I said, thinking of Carmel's words. *He likes you Daisy Jane, that man likes you.*

"How are you?"

"I'm fine," I said, suddenly wanting to tell him that I wasn't a protester after all, that I had been too scared to go to Pennsylvania to protest, but at the same time afraid I would cry from shame, and not wanting to put him in the position of having to comfort me, not wanting to give him that foothold in my life. "How are you?"

"It's a bad day," he said.

"Did you want to talk about it?" I said. He looked over at me and then at a bench near us. He sat down and I felt I ought to follow. It was bone cold but dry.

"I'm tired of talking about it actually. I'm tired of having the conversations with Jane and her doctors and her social worker and her physiotherapist. I'm tired of saying how I'm managing. It's a bad day," he said again. "I'm sorry."

We looked out at the water, which was now a leaden gray, with all the sodden leaves and duckweed trapped against the shore.

"Tell me you're not fine," he said. "Tell me it's not as easy as it looks to just be rid of your husband once and for all."

I felt weak then, a wave from my stomach down through my legs. "Easy?" I said.

"That came out wrong," he said. "God knows, I don't wish her dead, but it's death by a million paper cuts for me. There are days when it looks so much cleaner the other way. But I'm not looking for a pissing match. Did I mention this was a bad day?"

I moved my feet on the gravel beneath them, not even entirely sure what to say.

"I guess I'm just asking you to be honest as a way of stemming my pity party," he said. "Tell me the grass isn't greener."

I took a deep breath. "It's strange," I said. "I've never been hit in the face with a shovel before, but that's what it was like at first. When he died. I guess that's the shock of it. And now, I have to figure out how to finish everything by myself."

Everything, I thought. The leaves and the bills and Wednesday nights and the things we hadn't said and the things we had said to one another. There had been no goodbyes. The morning Arthur died, I had been in the shower when he left for work. I never actually said goodbye to him, not even for the day, let alone for always. I had thought about that over and over again the week of the funeral, standing near his coffin. I had said my goodbyes to him then, but I was sure they didn't count. It felt like someone getting converted over and over again, when it didn't seem to take. I had wondered whether since Arthur

was now outside time, maybe he would know that I would
have said goodbye, had I known. But maybe that was the
sedative they gave me to sleep.

"Do you miss him?" Henry asked.

I looked out at the water. Waves were coming from two
directions, colliding at the point in a confusion of ripples.
I wanted Henry to be my priest, to hear my confession.
He had been honest with me and I had no idea what his
motivation was. I had no idea whether Henry had any veneer
with anyone or whether what you saw was what you got. I
had no idea whether my sense of impropriety was mine or
his. I could answer Henry honestly or I could answer him
politely. If I answered him truly, would there be any going
back? If I didn't tell someone, honestly, would there be any
going forward? I didn't know. There are conversations that
people don't have, especially when they are not of the same
gender, and when they are both married to someone else.
But now I wasn't. It felt like a head rush as I spoke, like I had
been drinking and had lost the veneer of civilization I usually
wore.

"We had been married for thirty-nine years," I said. "We
were never going to be those ninety-year-olds holding
hands, making everyone swoon about our everlasting love.
But it was good and comfortable and now it's almost always
uncomfortable at the very best."

He nodded and I wanted him to say something but I didn't
know what. "You get into habits," I said. "You have ways of
doing things. I liked my comfortable life very much. I know

people want excitement but I never did. I never did."

"What I don't like is monotony," he said.

"Monotony doesn't hit you in the mouth like a shovel."

"No, but it kills you just the same," he said. "Do you think Arthur, do you think he wanted excitement?"

I needed the wind blowing straight at me in order to breathe. "Excuse me?" I said.

"I'm sorry, Daisy," he said. "I didn't mean—it's been a bad day."

I put my hand in my pocket and I found a stone and I held it in my hand and I ran my thumb over it. I could tell by the feel of it that it was limestone.

"Can I help?" I asked.

He smiled wryly. "I'm sure you could, but not the way I'd like help. Unless you have a magic wand."

"You could get away for a few days," I said.

"Where would I go?"

"You could go to New York."

"If it was New York I wanted, Daisy, I'd go and I'd thank you. But it isn't New York."

He fumbled around in his pocket, took a photograph out of his wallet and handed it to me. "I keep this picture of Jane in my wallet so I don't forget who she was, who she really is." It was a picture of Jane in a scarlet sundress and a sombrero, holding castanets and twirling so that her skirt stood out from her legs. "She dazzled me," he said. "I never expected to know anyone like Jane, let alone be married to her. Every day was fireworks with Jane."

"Arthur always called her a sparkplug."

"She was. She was that."

I turned and watched the lines of water rippling toward us, like carved wood block prints, so distinct the small waves were.

"The problem is that I don't remember that day anymore. I know it was in Mexico, before we even knew she was sick. But I don't remember that day or that Jane. I read somewhere that the body entirely regenerates new cells every seven years. It's been more than eight years since she was diagnosed."

We were sitting on the bench, bleeding all over each other, and I wasn't sure whether we were helping each other not drown or pulling each other farther down.

"What might you want?" I said.

"You know what I keep picturing," he said. "I think about the bees and when I put in a new frame. You start with a flat piece of board with a foundation on the bottom, a pre-shaped honeycomb pattern in wax. It saves the bees the bother of building their own base. I keep picturing someone pulling out this mess and giving me a fresh start, with a new established base. One that wouldn't get screwed up." He looked over at me. "How about you? What do you want?"

"I just want my son," I said and suddenly I knew that was true. "I want to keep him safe and see him more than once every few years. I wish he was seven again, and I'd tuck him into bed again, only this time I wouldn't skip any nights because I was tired or because he was too old to be tucked in. This time, I'd know that time passes too quickly, that soon he'd be on the other side of the world. I'd make sure I paid attention."

"Can I walk you home?" he said, standing up.

"Henry," I said, trying to keep my voice as light as I could. "You're a married man."

"I'm still capable of walking," he said.

"I think I'm not done here yet," I said. "I'm sorry it was a bad day."

"Me too."

I sat and watched as the ripples and waves got messed up together as the water got deeper.

I called Nick that night. He started telling me about his new girlfriend and I listened with my heart in my throat. "Any chance of you coming home anytime soon?" I asked when he had finished extolling the virtues of Allison.

"Is everything all right?" he asked.

"It's fine," I said. "I'm just not relishing the thought of Thanksgiving on my own."

"I thought you had that lady, that professor living with you."

"You know what I mean," I said. "And I don't know. Maybe she'll go to her sister's for Thanksgiving."

"Let me see what I can do."

"I'm not trying to make you feel guilty."

"I know. It's okay."

Wilma Subra. Theo Colborn. Rachel Carson. I said those

names to myself like a mantra, like something that kept me going. I had long heard people say that children needed role models, that girls needed to see women scientists, for instance. I had not been against the idea—it seemed reasonable—but neither did it seem entirely necessary.

And then, Carmel gave her presentation about women fracktivists. She started with Rachel Carson who had published *Silent Spring* in the '60s. She wasn't exactly a fracktivist, Carmel said, but she would have been. Theo Colborn was a doctor but that had happened late in life too, once her children were raised. Wilma Subra was a company president but she was a Sunday School teacher too and a Catholic.

I stayed in my seat after the class ended. You didn't have to have dreadlocks and piercings and tattoos. You didn't have to be twenty-six years old. Rachel Carson. Wilma Subra. Theo Colborn.

"Daisy Jane," Carmel said and I could tell she had already tried to get my attention. "You want to stay and help me make posters for the rally? I'm just going to finish them up here in the lounge and then I'll leave them in the office on the Commons."

"Okay," I said. I followed her out to the lounge and looked up at the dark sky visible through the skylights above us while she rummaged in her bag for markers. "She was a Sunday School teacher."

"She still is, I think," Carmel said, handing me rolled-up Bristol board. "If you mean Wilma Subra."

"But I'm a Sunday School teacher," I said. I took elastic bands off and held the board flat with my hands while Carmel's markers squeaked messages of hope and anger across the page. "Could I look after Aurora for you during the rally?" I said.

She looked up at me with disappointment.

"Carmel," I said. "I'm a housewife, not a scientist or a geologist. I don't even know what I'm doing for my presentation. So you don't have to be young. You still have to have something to offer."

"Honey," she said. "You don't see it, do you? You bring people together who would never meet otherwise and you make them at home together. You care about people and you care about this place. You care and it connects with your Sunday School teaching and your soup and everything."

"Sometimes I feel like I wasted everything," I said.

"Nothing's ever wasted. The question is how you use what you have, not how you get what you don't have."

"I don't think I can yell and scream," I said, and there was a catch in my voice.

"Do you know what my mom did on September 11? When the world was crashing in? I was in high school then. Lots of kids, their moms and dads picked them up, all scared and crying. My mom let us stay the day at school and then after school, she picked me and my brother up and we went down to the lake for a swim and a picnic. I remember that it was so quiet that day, with no planes in the sky, and my mom had brought us fried chicken, which was a treat. And my dad joined us after work and he rolled up his pants and waded in the water. It was the most extraordinary day. Because we knew exactly what had happened and we were all scared and sad, but my mom said that living normally was a political act, that living well meant we would not let the terrorists win."

"That's the first time you ever mentioned your mother," I said.

"She died when I was in twelfth grade. Ovarian cancer. And she took that on the same way. She wouldn't let us give in then either. We released butterflies at her memorial service.

"She was a housewife too, Daisy Jane. But she did something on September 11. It turned out she donated blood while we were at school and then she made a picnic for us. You remind me of her."

"What was her name?" I asked.

"Jennifer. Jenny Lear. And she taught Sunday School too."

Rachel Carson. Theo Colborn. Wilma Subra. Jenny Lear. My mantra was expanding. The slow underwater avalanche.

9
Fracking Soup

Class the next week was significantly different. Ben stood beside a man in a suit who carried the sleekest laptop I had ever seen. The class was fuller than it had ever been too and it crackled with energy as I came into the room and found my seat.

Carmel's eyes were bright and snapping.

"Who's that?" I asked her, nodding toward the man in the suit.

"Halliburton," she said. "He's come to tell us about the joys of fracking."

When the Halliburton man stood, hand on hip, talking with Ben as the class trickled in, I knew that I didn't like him but I also could remember the heart doctor Arthur had had. I hadn't liked the heart doctor—he was brusque and rude and short with us when we went for appointments after Arthur's first episode.

"I don't really care about his bedside manner, Daisy," Arthur had said to me, his legs swinging naked beneath his Johnny coat on the examining table when the doctor had left us alone for a minute and I had told Arthur that I wanted a second opinion, that I didn't like this doctor. "What I care about is that he can help me, that he knows hearts. And he does. I'm not looking to have coffee with him. I'm looking to stay alive to have more coffee."

Ironically, the doctor had taken Arthur off coffee at one of these appointments, but the lesson had been a good one for me. I watched the doctor and he was competent and skilled. I never liked him but he probably gave Arthur a couple more years he might not have had.

I wanted to give Mr. Halliburton a fair chance too. He showed a short video with farmers hugging fracking experts, tears in their eyes that they wouldn't be facing foreclosure after all, that they could keep farming their land and only sell the drilling rights. There was a mushroom cloud and ominous smoke from a nuclear power plant. There was a windmill standing still and solar panels at night. There was video of a coal-fired plant throwing more and more smoke into a sky already yellow with smog. There was a fine blue line drilling deep into the earth, and then back up again.

I tried to listen but the video didn't even show the rock fracturing. It was a thin blue elevator going down and up again. I found myself getting angry simply because the story had been so sanitized. And I wasn't the only one. I was surrounded by people whose anger was palpable and free. There were catcalls of *bullshit* from every corner of the darkened room.

I didn't say anything. I didn't call out one single bullshit, as satisfying as that would surely have been. It was not a word I had ever said before in my life.

When my mother was dying, she was a terrible, terrible

person. She said things I hope I will someday be able to forget, called us all names, was bitter to the last. But the thing was that she had always been bitter. The chaplain at the hospital took me aside and said, "In times of crisis, we don't become noble. We become more of who we are."

I thought of little Aurora toddling across my kitchen floor, her one eye on me. I had wondered whether my not going to blockade in Pennsylvania was me saying, "Yeah I just let it happen" and then I realized that no: in this crisis, it was okay to be myself; in fact, if the chaplain was at all right, it was impossible for me not to be myself.

I thought, for the thousandth time, about Carmel's words: "The question is how you use what you have, not how you get what you don't have." And so eventually I tuned out the shouting around me, turned a page in my book and started doodling a recipe for the next week's meal. I had already planned a tofu-ginger-kale soup, but I had a new idea. I would make a fracking soup. At first I imagined an inedible recipe—a kind of art installation, a way of shocking the crowd—stones and sand and a layer of motor oil. That felt exciting but I couldn't do it, for so many reasons—not least of which that I was scared that some of the ESL wives might misunderstand and actually eat it. And then I thought about a recipe I had made years before—with chunks of carrots and potatoes and barley and kale—it had been called Kitchen Sink Soup and Nick had called it Shipwreck. Could I make Shipwreck and call it Fracking Soup?

I could and I would.

I woke up nervous early on Tuesday morning. I started
chopping the vegetables and got the soup simmering,
except for the kale, which I would add a couple of hours
before people came. When Nick was little, I would employ
him to make a small sign that told guests what the soup of
the week was. No one ever let Nick forget the time he had
added gagging faces to a spring greens soup. I had kept up
the tradition, adding doodles of vegetables and grains to the
edges of each week's sign. I sat with my third piece of paper
in hand, doodling on the discarded versions.

This was a political statement. I thought of Reagan again:
All great change in America happens at the dinner table,
he had said. I tried to think whether we had ever before
had a dinner that was political in nature. We had rejoiced
in the freeing of the Iranian hostages under Carter. We had
cheered at the fall of the Berlin Wall together, but that was
not divisive, at least not among Americans. We had consoled
one another after Tiananmen Square, careful and aware that
our Asian guests could not speak openly. We clasped hands
and they held on longer than they needed to, I remember
that. We sat in shock on September 12, 2001, the skies far
too silent, but the need to gather so strong, grieving what
had happened so close to us. The Gulf War was probably
the closest thing: military and pacifists alike came to our
supper, and ended up sitting in different rooms or corners,

knowing somehow what was safe. It felt very good to be able to provide a place where both were welcome, where answers were not certain or divisive, even for just a couple of hours. Arthur and I had been Switzerland, neutral, not wearing team colors. My mother would say that was etiquette and it had worked for me for more than thirty-five years. To serve fracking soup had seemed a simple thing, but now, pen on paper, it was more complicated. Would I alienate people? Create tension? What was I hoping for anyhow?

I went up to the study which still felt like Arthur's. "Honey," I said quietly, closing the door behind me. "I've got a question for you." And then, out of nowhere, the tears fell. These were the kinds of times when Arthur had advised me, from the time I was a very young bride. Arthur had been raised properly by proper parents who loved him securely. The combination meant that Arthur could separate true etiquette from my mother's peculiar rules, could help me know what was appropriate and what was okay.

I sat in the chair across from his desk and I pretended with all my heart that he was there, listening, as he had done on many occasions before. It usually only took a word or two from Arthur to right my course; I hadn't needed long speeches or direction from him, nor was he likely to offer them.

I tried to imagine what he would say but it felt like I was making him into a puppet for what I wanted him to say, that I was as stuck as I had been.

"I don't want to make people feel condemned," I said,

thinking of Amos and his family. "I want them to feel comfortable in our house. I don't want them to think that Wednesday nights are a cover for me to stand on a soapbox."

Suddenly I could picture Arthur's face, amused, looking at me over his glasses, as if to say, "Yes, Daisy, I'm sure that they see you as the soapbox type."

And then, not Arthur but deeper in my being, the words came to me: *You've earned the right to speak. And you can spend that currency.* I went downstairs again and began to make the sign before I lost my way again. Lee came upstairs into the kitchen.

"Would I be in your way if I boiled the kettle?" she asked.

I shook my head. "Lee," I said, holding the pen still. "The soup I'm making for tonight, I'm calling it Fracking Soup."

It had taken millions of years for the Marcellus Shale to form, mountains rising and falling, a long slow avalanche of mud underwater in water so dense it was nearly without oxygen.

I gathered the shreds of kale I had chopped into a bowl and put it in the fridge. "People won't, they won't expect this from me."

"True."

"So, is it too political?"

She shrugged. "I wouldn't make them sign a petition before they get to eat or anything like that. But, it's something you're passionate about. Lots of people are, apparently. I think it's fine to share your story."

My stomach lurched. "My story?"

"You were just going to serve the soup?"

"I don't want to polarize Wednesday nights. I want people to be welcome."

"But do you want it to be a 'don't ask, don't tell' supper?"

"I feel like I'm supposed to be neutral."

"You're allowed to have an opinion and still make people feel welcome," she said and the kettle began to whistle. "Do you want tea?"

"No thanks."

She poured the water into the teapot.

"Maybe I should get Ben to talk," I said. Ben could give all sides of the argument.

She rolled her eyes.

"Or Carmel."

"Tell your story," she said.

There was never a set start and end time to Wednesday nights, and no magic moment when dinner was served or grace was said. Occasionally someone would tinkle cutlery on a glass to get everyone's attention to tell them about a concert or a new baby, someone getting tenure or a green card. At the last minute, I decided not to put a sign beside the soup for the first time in memory. More than a few people asked me what kind of soup it was and I replied vaguely, listing the ingredients. The room was buzzing with people—I was so glad Ben did not appear to be there—when

I decided it was time to talk. My mouth felt dry and my legs were shaky, so I leaned against a sofa for support. I took a spoon and a glass and rapped against it, almost hoping that it wouldn't work, that no one would hear. But the sound rang out crystal clear and the room fell almost instantly silent, with the exception of a voice in the corner jokingly saying, "Kiss...kiss."

"Sorry to interrupt," I said. My vision narrowed to a dark tunnel but I kept talking, as if I had to unravel what I had to say before I could stop. "We've had dinners here for thirty-five years and I've never done what I'm about to do now. You should know that. And that I'm nervous to do it now."

I could see, from the edge of my vision, Cecily step out of the kitchen. I saw Lee across the room and she gave me a nod.

"Some of you have asked what the soup tonight is. I usually label the soup, but I was worried that people would be offended if I labeled it without explanation."

"It's not meat, is it?" one girl called out.

"No, no. I promise it's not that. I'm calling this soup Fracking Soup and I thought I should explain a little bit. You've probably seen the signs around, saying no fracking. It's a complicated issue but I think it's one we need to talk about because it's going to affect all of us, whatever happens. This is our backyard. This is the ground we stand on."

"What is fracking?" someone asked.

"Drilling for gas," someone else replied.

"That's right," I said. "But it's drilling with high pressure and chemicals, fracturing rock deep beneath the surface. I wish Ben was here to explain it better but the more I've looked at it, the more I think it's something we all need to consider. There are compelling reasons to say no to it and there's a rally next week and I just wanted to start the discussion—and so I wanted to serve you this soup."

"It's delicious," someone called out.

"Thank you," I said, peeling myself off the sofa, shaking more than ever. That was not at all what I had hoped to say. I felt like I had squandered my one and only chance to speak up, that it might as well have been "Santa Claus Soup" at Christmas, thematic and not in any way radical. I felt tears coming to my eyes. I thought of Carmel and wondered if I had said, in effect, "I let it happen."

I went to the restroom, locked the door and wished everyone would go away but the weight of being a hostess intruded. I heard someone calling for me, soon afterward. I splashed water on my hot cheeks, fluffed my hair up and avoided looking at myself in the mirror.

It was Cecily. "I'm sorry to bother you," she said. "Do you have any butter? I can't see any in the fridge and I didn't bring any."

I shook my head. "I used the last of it on the onions for the soup. I didn't think."

"No problem," she said. "I'm not sure anyone will notice even."

"How so?"

"You got the room buzzing, girl," she said, patting my arm

and smiling.

I went back and stood in the shadow at the edge of the living room. I could hear bits of conversation and it was indeed louder than usual. I saw Henry across the room and he nodded at me and smiled, a steady smile that anchored me a little. And then Lee was at my elbow.

"Good work," she said.

I shook my head. "I don't know," I said. "I couldn't bring myself to say it was wrong."

"I don't imagine anyone thought this was an Amway party where you were promoting it."

I looked over at her. "Is Carmel here?" I asked.

She pointed at the front porch where the lights were on and we could see people gesturing. I sighed.

"It's not her house," Lee said. "She can say things you can't. Things you don't need to say."

"I wasn't just a coward, then?"

She gave me a teacherly look. "No, Turner, you weren't a coward. Now, go eat before the soup is all gone."

I walked back into the light of the room.

"Hello Queen Bee," said Henry. "You've got them buzzing tonight." Again, buzzing. But Queen Bee? I was more comfortable as worker. I knew that queens were not so much born as developed, but I did not know how. Nor was I about to ask him.

I felt my shoulders drop an inch or two, but I found a quiet chair in the kitchen and spooned soup into my mouth, trying to focus for a minute on the flavors and the heat, and to briefly forget the conversations around me.

The talk followed me. People came into the kitchen and joined me at the table, asking me questions and for my opinion. It felt like a barrier had been removed. I remembered Nick's friends whose parents wanted to be called by their first names, hearing Nick call them Tony and Sheila, instead of Mr and Mrs, as the rest of us were. Tony and Sheila were casual, easygoing, but I felt like something was lost in the informality. I liked Nick's friends calling me Mrs. T. I wasn't sure whether I liked the shift from hostess to being part of the discussion. It was not comfortable. On the other hand, I had never felt so involved on a Wednesday night before, never felt so much myself. Carmel had joined the talk in the kitchen and Henry stood, leaning against a doorway, listening. Carmel called me Daisy Jane and I looked over at Henry and saw surprise on his face.

The day of the rally, I said my mantra when I woke up with a knot in my stomach. I had mentioned the rally on Wednesday night at the supper, and over breakfast, I asked Lee if she wanted to join me.

"Sure," she said. "What time is it?"

"Four-thirty," I said, marveling that her decision could be that easy. It would be good to have someone to go with, Theo Colborn to my Wilma Subra, Thelma to my Louise.

The protest was late in the afternoon and the hearing would

be in the evening. It made me think of my wedding. My mother had insisted on a late afternoon society wedding— four o'clock— and the waiting around for it had nearly killed me. She had planned a luncheon for the bridesmaids and me but none of us were hungry and none of us wanted to disturb our curls. I remember we sat and watched the snow fall outside and listened to music for much of the afternoon, and the girls had asked me what it was like to get married and where we were going on our honeymoon and I had doodled my name-to-be on a pad of paper, and had toyed with the idea of reverting to Jane. Arthur had only found out that my name was Jane when we had the banns read in church and he said it at the rehearsal, but as he said to me afterwards, "It almost felt like I was marrying someone other than the person I planned to marry." Who was this Jane, he said. I wasn't sure. I sat with the girls in my heavy dress, and patted my muff as if it was a pet, and I wasn't sure how I felt. Excited, I suppose, and a bit nervous.

That was how I felt now, only I was honest enough to admit that it was actually in reverse: more nervous than excited. I suppose that's what I was then too. I had wanted a summer wedding with daisies, but it made more sense for me to join Arthur in Chicago. I had settled for a veil that had lace flowers all over it, flowers you could believe were daisies.

And the rally wasn't what I had expected at all. There were signs and there was chanting but this was Ithaca and so there was music and laughing and there was coffee, stores offering us use of their restrooms. There were people

I hadn't seen since Arthur died, and there were hugs. The crowd was mostly young but there were people older than me there too—there were dozens of strollers but there was an occasional wheelchair too. I walked near the center of the crowd, with Lee at first, and we were joined by her ESL student Weng who linked her arm with Lee's. And then I was stopped by the tattooed man from my class and I waved Lee and Weng on ahead of me. I began to see that there were a number of people from Wednesday night in the crowd. I felt tears prickle in my eyes at the idea of it. I found myself introducing people and there were handshakes, juggling of signs and banners. We walked through the Commons together and we filled the space as music fills a space, simply with its presence. I found myself smiling. I loved this place. No one had asked my age or laughed at me for being older. If anything, I felt like people were delighted to have older people among them; we were ahead of the curve, giving credibility and depth and wisdom to what they were doing and saying.

A few minutes later, I saw Carmel out of the corner of my eye. "Excuse me," I said to Nate, the man from class, and I slid through the crowd to Carmel. Her father was walking with her, pushing Aurora's stroller, which was decked out in banners and balloons.

"Thanks for coming," she said, giving me a one-armed hug.

"I'm glad I did," I said. "I really am."

Someone ahead was calling her name and she slipped through the crowd, holding her sign above her head. I fell in step with her father.

"So, you are a fracktivist after all," he said, smiling.

"And so are you," I said, right back. I was fully aware of the fact that I felt grateful to walk with someone my own age, even if I wasn't sure about his name.

"Carmel told me you lost your husband this year," he said as we walked.

I nodded. "May," I said. I hated that expression, "lost your husband." He wasn't lost; I knew exactly where Arthur was buried.

"I know what it's like," he said.

I nodded again. He did. Beyond that, what could I say about this club we shared? I knew the answers to the catechistic questions by now: does it get easier? Sometimes. Does it still catch you off-guard, grief? Yes. Is it linear? No. Do you have more good days than bad days now? Do you still wake up and listen for him snoring down the hall? Do you know where the snow tires are? That eavestroughs need cleaning? That people suspect you of husband thievery? That sometimes it is every bit as fresh as the very first day and other days you think you're getting the hang of it?

We reached the legislature and people pooled around the building. Carmel was one of those who stood on the steps and spoke, and I fed Aurora Cheerios and I felt so proud of Carmel. And then, across the lawn, I saw Henry, leaning against a tree. I don't know whether he felt my eyes on him, but as I watched him, he glanced over and his eyes met mine.

"Well," Carmel said, coming back to walk with me after the

rally. "They came for Amos's family and now they've come for me. The frackers. It turns out they leave an offer in your mailbox and then you're supposed to dream about what you'll do with the money and they come back a few days later to give you the actual contract to sign."

"I'm sorry."

"It also turns out that abstract money is easier to turn down than real money."

I was surprised. I had seen her protest and curse. I had just heard her impassioned words.

"I keep thinking about what we could do with the money. We could pay off the mortgage we took out when we built the second house and got the new cider press. We could breathe easy and sleep at night."

"Could you?" I said.

"Well, if it was as clean and simple as their letter suggests, sure, we could." She sighed. "Sadly, it's not. But it helps me anyhow to know that it's tempting. I told my brother we would just rip up any letter that came, but we didn't. We sat and drank and talked about it—tried to make it work, tried to make ourselves believe maybe we had been wrong, that maybe the drilling was deep enough, that maybe we could persuade them to clean up the tailing ponds on our property and it would be okay. But no matter how much we drank or talked, we couldn't bring ourselves to do it. The problem is, what if all our neighbors do, what if it doesn't matter that we held out, that we kept our principles intact. What if our water gets poisoned and we're still mortgaged to the hilt. What then?"

"What can we do?"

"Thank you, Daisy Jane. For the we. I don't know. What do you think?"

"Want me to bring some fracking soup over and you can invite your neighbors?"

"You and soup."

"Or you could get them drunk on cider."

She laughed. "Justin told me they're starting a group. What's my neighborhood? Is it just our ridge? Is it the whole watershed? The whole Marcellus Shale?"

There was always a smell about church bazaars that was always exactly the same. People brought different things each year, but somehow the smell—stale, yellowed, fusty— was always the same. Every house had a different smell to it, but I wondered as Cecily and I walked among our fellow parishioners' stuff whether unused, unloved things took on the scent of decay.

Some people loved searching for treasures at a rummage sale, but the smell always made me feel sad. It was a good place to pick up bowls for Wednesday nights and I found a couple of new ones and a tablecloth that would fit my dining room table, but I also saw things at the bazaar this year that I knew were in my cupboards, things I didn't want, hadn't seen in years: I felt guilt on top of my sadness, and I retreated to the kitchen where we sold jams and Styrofoam trays of sugar cookies and shortbread. These at least smelled clean and buttery and good.

Maybe, I thought, as I sipped on a cup of burned coffee, maybe my heart would lighten if I got rid of my own decaying stuff.

I thought about glacial deposits as I looked around my house later. It was not a bad metaphor for all the stuff we had accumulated. I was in the dining room when Lee walked in.

"Your son called," she said. "He said to tell you he's coming home for Thanksgiving."

I put my hands over my face, afraid I would burst with joy. "Thank you," I said. "I keep meaning to ask you: you are staying here for Thanksgiving, aren't you? Will you join us for turkey?"

"Are you sure? You don't want me out so your son can have his room back?"

"He's too tall for the basement," I said. "And yes, you are most welcome to join us. Please do—unless you have a better offer."

"My sister had offered," Lee said. "But I kind of overdosed on Arizona last winter."

"Then it's settled."

"Thank you, Daisy."

She walked into the kitchen.

"Help yourself to the pie," I said. "It's from my church bazaar."

I stood with my hands on the back of a dining room chair,

rooted with happiness. I looked around the table. I could see Nick there laughing. I could see Lee and me. But I could see Arthur too. I wondered whether Lee would be enough of a change for us to banish Arthur's presence. Cecily went to her mother's every Thanksgiving. I wondered about Carmel, whether she would have plans, whether her brother and father would come as part of the package.

I wondered too whether Nick would see changes in me, seven months widowed. I looked in the mirror across from me. My face, my hair, everything looked the same to me, almost disturbingly so. My life had been fracked, blown apart from deep inside, and yet, I couldn't see any evidence on the surface.

I had heard that some people made radical changes after major life events—cutting off their hair, getting a tattoo, going gray. I wanted some outward sign that everything was not business as usual as it had been for almost forty years. And then, I knew what to do. Nick had laughed at the gold shag carpet we had throughout the dining room and living room—"It's so dated, it was retro ten years ago." I would have it pulled it up. Before Thanksgiving.

"Lee," I said. She didn't answer; she had gone back down stairs. I went downstairs and knocked on her door.

"What's going on?" she asked, opening the door.

I folded my arms in front of me. "What would you think," I said, "about me getting rid of the carpet upstairs? Before Nick comes home."

She laughed. "He might not recognize the house."

"I don't know if I can get anyone at such short notice."

"Get someone? Daisy, all you need is a good knife and a couple of rolls of duct tape. We could have the carpet out by supper time."

By supper time.

"Is this what you want?" she asked. "Because you could empty out the china cabinet while I go pick up the things we need, and then we could move the furniture out."

I nodded. I wanted change, visible change. "We might have the right kind of knife already," I said. "In Arthur's work room."

"Well, let me get changed and I'll have a look."

I went upstairs, dazed, and looked at the carpet again. I took a deep breath and opened the china cabinet. We had four sets of dishes—our good china, our everyday china, Arthur's mother's china and my grandmother's china—as well as the stacks of bowls and spoons I used for Wednesday evenings. I had moved all the cups and saucers to the kitchen table by the time Lee came upstairs, in jeans, brandishing a utility knife.

"All we need is duct tape," she said. "But I was thinking you should have a look at what's underneath before we really get started. Just in case it's plywood. You don't want to have Thanksgiving dinner on plywood." She bent down at the corner of the room and looked up at me. "Here goes nothing," she said and I crouched beside her as she wiggled her fingers under the edge of the carpet, gently pushing it up, before peeling the corner back. "Good news," she said.

"You've got hardwood floors under here."

And it was beautiful hardwood. I unloaded the china cabinet, and Lee and I shuffled furniture from the dining room to the living room and then the other way, while she ripped at the carpet with her utility knife, and I took the strips she had cut away, rolled them up and bound them with tape. The floor beneath was thick was dust, but beneath that, the finish was still good. There was one area of water stain in the living room, and I wasn't sure whether it was from Nick's old fish tank or my plants, but it would be hidden under a couch anyhow. I swept the floor and washed it, while Lee carried out rolls of carpet to the curb for trash day on Monday.

We ordered in Chinese and sat at the dining room table, too tired and achy to put the china back in the cabinet, almost too tired to talk.

"Thank you," I said. My voice sounded different in the uncarpeted room. "I think we should have done this years ago."

"That's what I thought when I pulled up my carpet before I sold the house," Lee said. She handed me a fortune cookie and broke hers open. "'Your ability to accomplish tasks will follow with success.' Not well written but true. What does yours say?"

I cracked mine and pulled out the paper. "'Today is the tomorrow we worried about yesterday.'"

10
Three Sisters Soup

We had only ever been able to have the one child but he was more than enough for me. I had both wanted and feared a daughter, but there was an ease with a son that I had never experienced with my mother and could not have imagined experiencing. It was something like being on holiday much of the time. Nick had a sense of lightness about him, a sense of humor and joy—other women talked about empty nest syndrome when their children left home, but I knew some of their children and frankly I thought I might celebrate bidding farewell to some of them. Not so with Nick.

I had tried not to smother him, not to make his interests my interests. I had tried to give him space and still he had moved to Singapore. At some level, I believed he needed to move away from us, even though I had done everything I could to make that unnecessary.

I had worked very hard, too, at not bugging him about girlfriends and asking for grandchildren. I had listened to his stories and welcomed him home. I had never made him feel guilty about living so far away. These were accomplishments of the mother of an adult child that were kind of like properly wiring a house or grinding your own flour: no one would notice or laud such accomplishments and yet they could make a big difference.

I had not had to ask Nick to come home when his father died: he was home within eighteen hours, red-eyed and remorseful, mine to hold. And then, four days later, he had been back on the plane.

It felt like a weakness to ask him to come home for Thanksgiving. I did have Lee there. I wouldn't be alone. I could go to someone else's house if I chose to make my availability known. I could travel to South Carolina to Arthur's family, be one of twenty guests at a groaning table.

But when he said he could come, my heart sang within me with true thanksgiving. I ordered a fresh turkey at the market and I bought the fingerling potatoes he loved and I asked Carmel where I could buy her apple cider, and I invited her for Thanksgiving supper—she said her dad and brother had gluttonous plans she was glad to escape, plans involving the television, fried chicken and sweatpants—and I made pies and pies and I left my uncertainty about my presentation aside for the week. The fracking world could wait for my boy to come home.

"I want to talk with you about what you want from the house," I said to Nick when he called to tell me that he couldn't get a flight before Thanksgiving Day itself but that he would stay a few extra days.

"Are you moving?" he said.

"No," I said. "I'm just going through things. We have four sets of china."

"I don't want china."

"But what if you get married?" I said.

"I still don't want china. I have dishes." We had, obviously, inherited our dishes, but there was no apparent heir for them.

"How many dishes?" I asked.

"More than enough," he said. "You're getting morbid."

I didn't think I was. I called Arthur's sister in Memphis to find out whether she wanted her mother's china.

"Daisy honey," she said. "You know I got Grandmommy's china and silver, plus what I got when I got married. I'm drowning in china here already."

"If I were to find a good home for it, would anyone be upset?" I said. "I mean, what about Paige, would she like it?"

"She's like Nick. Says no one has china anymore."

I was walking through the parking lot at the grocery store where I had bought last-minute things—cream, chocolate and bread—and I was jubilant at the thought that Nick's plane was in the air now when I heard the purr of a vehicle alongside me. Henry opened his window.

"Hop in," he said. "I'll give you a lift."

"Really no," I said. "Thank you, Henry, but no. My car is just over there."

He let the engine idle. I thought of shale gas and wasted fuel and I felt guilty. I put my hands in my pockets.

"I was going to ask you whether you wanted to join us for Thanksgiving," he said. "You've fed us on so many occasions."

I felt guilty, that the truth was a shield I was hiding behind, rather than something I could hold out openly. "My son—Nick—is coming home. And I have Lee and a few other friends joining us. It's very kind of you to ask, though."

"I didn't want you to be alone at Thanksgiving," he said.

"Thank you," I said, putting my hand on his forearm and then taking it back quickly. It was like thinking about breathing—you could do it automatically unless you thought about it—this was a gesture I would do to anyone, wouldn't I? And yet, it seemed like inhaling when you should exhale, something that made you gasp and a little dizzy. "How is Jane?" I asked quickly.

"She had a terrible night last night—she's at the hospital right now, having tests. I was just filling her prescription."

"I'm sorry," I said and my heart calmed within me. "Is there something I can do to help?"

"Well," he said, his fingers tracing lines on the center of the steering wheel. "That's just it. In line work, there's always a mechanical solution. It's like when you have a garden hose and you turn it on but the water isn't coming out—you trace it back and find the kink in the hose, or the leak, or the problem with connection. You just need to figure out what you're missing."

He paused and I tried to figure out whether my growing anxiety was from the fuel he continued to burn or from the conversation.

"When Jane got sick, I went into the first meeting with the doctors with my work boots on—ready to figure it out.

But that's not how MS works and not the system either. You wait and see what happens. Drove me nuts. I talked with the doctors, tried to figure out what we were missing, what would make things work again. Probably all the pieces were there, are there, but we just know electricity better than we know the human body. I kept thinking that if only we did this right or that right, we'd be able to fix her up good as new, sparkling and crackling. Only there's a leak in the line somewhere and we have no idea where.

"I thought the world worked that way. Cause and effect. You probably think I'm an idiot, but there's something beautiful about a world that operates like that."

"There is," I agreed and we were silent together a minute. "So, I suppose we won't see you tonight?"

He shook his head.

"Do you want me to send you over some soup? It's the Three Sisters soup, you know, in honor of the native Americans."

He shook his head again and I was tempted to put a hand on his forearm again but I didn't.

"Happy Thanksgiving, Daisy," he said.

"Happy Thanksgiving."

I stopped at the cemetery on the way home. We had purchased plots there at the same time as we drew up our will, after Nick was born. We had been through the rigmarole with my mother who had refused to admit she was getting older until the dementia had taken her hostage. We had been through the chaos of what it meant for her to die without leaving behind a will, and we had learned from this. I was glad that everything had been taken care of when Arthur died too. I had friends who said that planning a funeral was as daunting as planning a wedding, but neither actually had been for me. My mother had done everything when I was married, and having pre-paid and pre-planned the funeral, I found there was surprisingly little to be done, not as much as I wished anyhow. I had wanted to make sandwiches, to actually do something, but people laughed at this impulse and wanted me to be still. As if I could. I soaked in the bath every night and then scrubbed it out thoroughly. And then, Nick was there, too briefly, and then he was gone again.

I missed both of them—Arthur who had always been there and Nick who was never there enough. I wondered whether Nick had moved halfway around the world because of the opportunities there or to be away from us, as I had needed to move away from my mother. And whether that us was Arthur, me or both of us.

I felt like maybe I should look at the date carved into the tombstone, still freshly carved, barely softened by a season's rain, and maybe confess my sins. As I walked out to Arthur's grave, with a space ready for my name to be carved and my body to be laid to rest, I thought about telling him that Nick was coming home, but when I got there, it all seemed like something beyond words and I just stood there and let a wave of emotion roll over me and then I stamped my foot hard on the ground.

"I might need a doorstop."

"Nick."

"That's about all they'd be good for to me. If you don't need them, go ahead."

"And you don't want the china."

"It would make a terrible doorstop."

"I thought this would be easier with you here," I said. "Smart aleck."

"I'd like Dad's chess set," he said. "The one he got in Iceland. And don't throw out my rock collection." At about the age of six, Nick had collected rocks everywhere we took him, to be just like his father. His collection ranged from fossils and semiprecious stones to large pea gravel he had collected near train tracks. Arthur had been so happy to see Nick collecting rocks that he hadn't had the heart to explain which ones mattered.

"Do you want me to send them to you?" I asked. "And what about the posters in your room?"

"Dr. Henshall said she liked them," he said. "She can keep them there. You're not moving or anything, are you?"

I shook my head. "I'm just simplifying."

"You got rid of his clothes, right?"

I nodded.

"Good," he said. "I don't know that there's anything else besides the chess set that I want. I'm not exactly a collector."

I was. I had the china horse collection and the silver spoons we started collecting when we got married and went to Taughannock Falls for our honeymoon. I had the four sets of china. I had all of Nick's toys. I had cookbooks and more cookbooks. I had sets of aprons and placemats and cloth napkins. I had our Christmas ornaments and my parents' Christmas ornaments. I had every craft Nick had ever made, every drawing he had ever made in school. I had albums of photographs and carousels of slides. I had camping equipment and boxes of sewing patterns. I had Arthur's rocks and Nick's rocks and even some of my own. I had bottles of sea glass and bags of shells. I had mason jar rings and board games. I had my maternity clothes from 1973. I had pillow cases and sheets and flannel sheets and wool blankets. I had punch bowls and crock pots. I had jelly molds and Bundt pans. I had a baby walker and a crib and a cat carrier. I had my wedding dress and hats in boxes. I had sheet music and cross country skis and a fondue pot. I had rug hooking kits and macramé. I had a jar of buttons from my grandmother and confederate coins from my grandfather. I had rows of National Geographics. I had shelves of paint cans and varnish. I had my own childhood dollhouse and furniture ready for a daughter.

Nick had been the executor of his father's will. It had pleased me that Arthur trusted him that much; he should— Nick had always been a whiz with money and details—but I knew it had been a step for Arthur to acknowledge it. Nick had retrieved the will from our lawyer's office when he came home for the funeral and he told me what I already knew: that the will, like mine, was very simple. Arthur had left everything to me. It would take time to work out the transfer of stocks to my name and the insurance claims, and there would still be taxes to take care of next year. Nick told me I could continue to live as usual, that I would be fine.

Nick had set up an appointment with our lawyer when he was home. Given the shortness of his visit, we had agreed to meet on Black Friday.

I walked out of the lawyer's office, dazed, and sat in the passenger seat of the car, having handed my keys to Nick. My hand felt naked and there was no disguising the fact that I had worn a ring for nearly forty years. I could feel the indent of the ring, even now that my salt swelling had subsided. It was one thing to keep my ring on after Arthur died—when did you take something like this off?—but it was another to put it back on again. And right now, especially, I felt guilty.

"You said I'd be fine," I said. "But we don't have a mortgage or anything."

Nick grinned. "The old man made sure you'd be taken care of."

"This is more than fine, Nick."

"Hey," he said and patted my knee, awkwardly. "It's okay. You don't have to decide what to do with it today."

"Okay," I said. He started the car and I groped for my seatbelt. "I could come to visit you in Singapore."

"I'd like that," he said.

We drove and my eyes blurred. I had never added up the

insurance money and I had not known that the university held a policy on Arthur too. "Could I, could I give some of the money to the school, in his name?"

"Of course you could. The only thing—and you have to be aware I'm not a disinterested adviser, but I would honestly say this to any of my clients—is that you should take your time. Do the math—what you need, what you might need, what you want. Money gives you options and you need to think about what you really want to do with this opportunity. Right now, though, what you probably need is to forget about it for a bit and just let it settle in. Do you want to go for a hike?"

We stopped at the house and got changed out of our meeting clothes.

"I know what I want," I said, when we got back in the car. "More than all this insurance money. I'd rather have your dad back."

"He'd be happy to know that," Nick said, swinging the car out. "Since he thought you were trying to kill him with tofu and all that."

He knew how to make me laugh, that son of ours who was our most precious legacy.

It was a cold day, with a brisk wind coming from the north and crashing into the side of the mountains. We went out to Taughannock Falls. It was three-quarter mile walk from the parking lot to the base of the falls themselves. The path ran slightly uphill and the walk back would be easier. One side of the gorge was covered with cedars and evergreens while the other supported sugar maples and other trees that had shed papery leaves at our feet, littering the trail that was crushed shale rock. We usually knew what we would see at the falls, by the force of the river that flowed from it, but occasionally we would be surprised by a torrent when we expected a trickle, or vice versa. The walls of the canyon were dizzyingly high and birds of prey often soared on thermals high above us, winter or summer. As we walked, Nick told me one of his teachers had once told his class, on a field trip, about a sudden flash flood that had ripped through the valley, washing out the road by the lake, the roar of the falls audible from the far side of the lake itself. "I used to stop before crossing the bridge every time, look at the falls and make sure it wasn't about to carry me off." Taughannock dropped in a single 200-foot cascade. I couldn't imagine such force and fury.

I saw a few gray hairs in Nick's sideburns and at his temples, hairs I had not noticed before.

"I saw the signs you were telling me about," he said. "The fracking signs. It's a big deal, huh?"

I told him about the offer for mining rights on Amos's and Carmel's farms.

"And you're still taking the course? With Carmel?"

"I am."

"Is it you, Mom?" he asked, bending down to pick up an

empty water bottle from the trail. "Is it really you? Or is it Dad?"

"How do we ever know anything like that for sure?" I said. "I know if it wasn't for the fact that it's an issue right here and if it wasn't for your father, I probably wouldn't be taking the class. But it feels like it's mine to do, mine to figure out right now."

"Sometimes I come back," he said. "And I see someone I went to high school with or even to college—I told you I saw Brooks in the airport the other day, right?—and I think wow, people still live here." He looked around. "No offense. I mean, it's just that it's been a really long time that I've been gone and I know my neighborhood and the good restaurants and people know me there, and it just seems like maybe everyone has moved on, or should have moved on. It's weird to come back and still know this place, but not really know it."

I knew what he meant. That was how I felt about Carolina.

"This is my place," I said. "And I care about it a whole lot."

He bent down again and picked up a newspaper, wedged among a pile of decaying leaves. "If people in Singapore saw this place, saw all the trash, they wouldn't believe people cared."

I took the water bottle from him. "We're doing the best we can," I said.

"I'm sorry about your friend last night," he said. "Sometimes I think I should move back here and help you out."

"What I wish," I said, putting the bottle into a recycling bin, "is that travel could be instant. So, I could come to see you when I felt like it and you could come home for Wednesday nights."

"You're still doing that?" he laughed.

I punched him in the arm. "They wouldn't let me stop if I wanted to. Which I don't." We reached the falls and stood watching the water tumble straight down from far above us. "But you don't need to help me out," I said. "I'm doing all right."

"I wasn't sure," he said. "You seemed pretty lost for a while."

"Darling," I said. "You try being married for almost forty years and then being on your own again."

"I don't know if I have forty years," he said, and suddenly I was prickled with anxiety. It was one thing to contemplate my own mortality and quite another to think that my son was old enough to wonder whether he was more than halfway through his life. Arthur had been sixty-two, only 26 years older than Nick was now. "Plus," he said, and there was Nick, beneath the gray hairs and the worry. "Who would want to be married to me for forty days, let alone forty years?"

"I have a friend," I said and he threw his arm around me.

"I'm frozen," he said. "Honestly I am. I live in tropical-land now. I've lost my edge."

"Turkey sandwiches and football?" I asked.

"Do you know what we have for Thanksgiving in Singapore, we expats?" he said. "Oysters and durian. And then a round of beach volleyball. I'm dying for turkey sandwiches and football."

"Do you see the layers in the rock?" I said.

"Oh God," he said. "Not you too. Seriously, Mom, I'm freezing."

"This is a little thing. You remember how we always said it looked like the rocks in the river and at the edge were manmade, like someone had carved them?"

He nodded.

"Apparently it's a natural thing after all, but they say that because these kinds of fractures already happen in the shale, if they do hydraulic fracturing here, it may cause the natural fractures to connect and make a kind of canal so that all the fracking fluids can flow directly into the groundwater."

"Can we go now?"

"Yes, honey. We can."

The hills were bare but the bones of the trees were beautiful as we walked back to the car. We came out of the gorge at the parking lot and it was suddenly ten degrees warmer.

"Thanks for picking up trash, Nick," I said. "And for coming home."

"If she wasn't an apple farmer, I'd think about it," he said with a smile I wished I could see every day.

When he left for the airport, he gave me a hug. "I'm proud of you, Mom," he said. "And Dad would be too."

It was a quick flip-flop of emotions and I didn't know what to feel. I put my arms out to give him a hug and he smelled like Nick and I held him longer than I was planning on, just to keep breathing him in.

"He's cute, your son, Daisy Jane," Carmel said at class on

Thursday. "Too old for me, but still cute."
     "That he is," I said.

11
Oyster Mushroom Soup

The secret we never tell tourists is that it often snows in November here. And if it doesn't, there are gray days that last for weeks. People stumble upon Ithaca like it's the promised land and they wonder why everyone doesn't live here. These were the days that would have explained why to them.

And this was one of those days. I made it to class, against my better judgment, sliding along roads that were glazed with ice. I told myself that if the car gave me any trouble climbing Fall Creek, I would turn around and come back home but I made it up the hill without my wheels balking and so I decided I would go to class.

Carmel came in ten minutes late and slipped in beside me. The first presentation was on rock types and it was the second time in the whole term that I actually had any foreknowledge of what anyone was talking about. I had helped Arthur with his handouts for first year classes on many occasions and the rock types had stayed in my mind. It was a relief to know that something had stuck.

I heard Carmel's phone buzz beside me and she glanced at it and swore under her breath. I looked over at her as she typed a reply.

"County road's closed," she said to me at the break. "Black

ice. I can't get home tonight."

"Come stay with us," I said.

"My dad's going to keep Aurora overnight," she said.

"Then it's settled."

She grinned. "A sleepover! Maybe you can teach me to make soup."

I might have smiled. Sometimes I had to work hard to remember what it was to be that young, to remember times before I knew what I knew so well now. I remembered my first cookbook, remembered watching Julia Child on PBS— that was how I learned to chop onions correctly. I hadn't been hatched with all the knowledge. I had accumulated it here and there. My mother had thrown away her chicken carcasses and I remember Arthur's cook being aghast as I carried the bones to the garbage to dump them. She had stopped me and shown me how to make stock, had told me how the boiling process killed any germs off. I had picked up tips from the market vendors and from Cecily, from trial and error. It was funny that some little children thought of me as the soup lady because it certainly wasn't the only meal I made. I read cookbooks with imagination, trying to decide whether I thought the flavors would work or not, making substitutions as I went.

But Carmel's mother had died when she was still a teenager and had been sick before that. Carmel confessed that soup was more often ramen noodles even than canned soup.

"I was going to make a mushroom soup this week just for us," I said. "I got some lovely oyster mushrooms at the market."

"I would love that."

Lee was waiting up in the kitchen when we walked in. "The roads are closed tonight so she's going to stay over."

Lee stood up. "I'm glad you're home. There have been nonstop sirens out there tonight."

"It was bad," I agreed. "Do you want some tea, Carmel?"

"I just boiled the kettle ten minutes ago," Lee said.

"I'd love some," Carmel said.

While the water reheated, I went upstairs to make up the bed for Carmel in our old bedroom. There were sheets on the bed, but I wasn't sure they had been changed since Nick had slept there. As I took the sheets off the bed, I held them to my nose to see if I could smell him at all, but there was nothing, only the scent of fabric softener. Maybe I had changed the sheets. I could hear the hish of sleet against the roof as I spread new sheets over the bed and pulled the comforter over top.

As I walked down the stairs, I could hear them talking.

"I think those were the same reasons I used to keep Aurora," Carmel said. "But I understand. Some days more than others."

"And I sometimes wonder what would have happened if I had kept him," Lee said.

My mother had often rebuked me sharply for listening in on adult conversation where I wasn't welcome. I wondered what had opened the conversation to such depths in five minutes. I remembered when I had been a girl in boarding school, taking the train back to North Carolina from New York each summer. I remember the conversations I had on that train, deeper than any I had with any of my girlfriends during the school year. I remembered the young man who invited me to stand between the cars to smoke with him and the things I had been able to say to people I would likely never see again. I had told him my name was Jane and it was like a secret identity. Although my secrets weren't revelations, it was still freeing to speak them aloud as the wheels bumped over the tracks.

If I had heard rightly, Lee had had a child at some point. And had presumably given him up for adoption. There was silence in the next room and I thought about creeping back up the stairs and coming down more loudly, and then Lee stood to make the tea, and they talked about the weather and laughed at something. I found the floorboard that creaked in the hallway and stepped on it, rocking my foot back and forth so that it made a certain sound, and then I walked forward into the kitchen and found my seat.

I looked over at Lee who sat with her hair down, iron gray, on her back, and I wondered, not for the first time, what the cost had been to her, having an academic career in the 1960s. I also felt a bit miffed, both that Lee had confided in my friend, and that Carmel had been the one to be able to elicit—apparently effortlessly—Lee's secrets when I, in knowing her for more than thirty-five years and living with her for several weeks, had not.

"Tea, Daisy Jane?" Carmel asked.

I could see Lee look inquisitively at the name, perhaps dismissing it as a slang pet name and I wondered how long she would live with me, whether this was a train relationship where everything could come out, or whether it was more prudent to keep one's cards close to one's chest.

"Sure," I said and held out my tea cup. We drank tea and talked about class until Lee excused herself for the night.

"So, you want to learn to make soup?"

I pointed her to a drawer that had aprons in it. She found a pink and brown bib apron and put it on, looking both amused and nervous. I was amused to think I was Julia Child to Carmel. She washed her hands and wiped them on the apron.

"So," she said.

"So," I said and handed her a paper bag filled with oyster mushrooms. "These are the mushrooms. Have a smell."

She reached for the bag and opened it to her nose. I like the smell of mushrooms. They're earthy and they smell pretty much exactly like what they are. They also smell a bit like oysters—it's a fresh smell.

She looked inside. "These look like the ones I use," she said. "I cultivate mushrooms for the apple trees."

"Pour them out here," I said. "You can chop them."

"Should I wash them?"

"Mushrooms are like sponges," I said. "I usually just wipe them clean with a fresh damp dishcloth." I reached into the drawer for a cloth as I heard the rubbery tumble of mushrooms on the counter.

I wet the cloth and handed it to her. She turned each mushroom like a precious object, taking as much time on one as I might have on the whole jumbled batch.

"Tell me if I'm telling you too much," I said, handing her a knife and a cutting board.

"Assume I know nothing," she said.

"Like me and my computer."

She laughed. "Exactly."

"Okay," I said. "The part under the mushroom is called the gills. Double-check that there are no chunks of dirt or anything in any of the mushrooms. No? Good. Now, you cut the little roots off the mushrooms—yes, just like that. And now, I usually cut them into smaller chunks so that they will sit flat in the pan and so that everyone will get some mushrooms and no one will get a big piece."

"Actually," she said, "I do have my great-grandfather's recipe for mushrooms. We found his notebook two years ago in the shed, behind a filing cabinet. Trevor and I talked to some horticulturalists at the university and some other apple growers and we figured out what his recipes were for."

"What they were for?"

"Compost tea, growing mushrooms on wood chips around the base of the trees, that kind of thing."

"You grow mushrooms for the trees?"

She nodded. "But that certainly won't happen in a polluted, fracked water table. It'll kill any good bacteria in the soil and then we'll have to spray. My midwife told me interventions caused more interventions. It's like that. Take an epidural for pain and you're more likely to need a C-section. It'll slow the labor down."

I had always been grateful that I lived in a time when doctors knew how to safely deliver babies one way or the other, but I had been afraid of what I heard about spinals they gave for pain and so I had ridden the wave, knowing that if it became a crisis, someone could intervene.

But this was no crisis requiring intervention. It was only our appetite for fossil fuel that was creating the problem.

"They're good for you too, oyster mushrooms," I said. "They reduce cholesterol. Although Arthur always liked his soup with thick cream so it kind of undid the good, I figured."

"Arthur was your husband."

"Yes. He was." I took a deep breath. I didn't have any space for Arthur at the moment.

I got out a soup pot and some butter and an onion. I began to melt the butter in the pot.

"Some people use olive oil," I said. "But I always think butter goes with mushrooms. Here, pass them over." She lifted the whole cutting board and I swept the pale gray-brown mushroom pieces into the butter where they sizzled. "Do you want to stir them?" I said. "Or do you want to chop more vegetables?"

She opted for stirring and I chopped the onion and added it quickly to the pan. "Some people add garlic or other vegetables, but I just like it when the mushroom can shine."

"Metaphorically speaking, right?"

"That's right. Now you add chicken stock or vegetable

stock—a couple of cups."

"You use instant?"

"Sure. Sometimes."

I added some white wine and a shot of soy sauce, a few turns of the pepper grinder and a sprig of thyme from the pots I had moved in from the porch before the first frost.

"And there you go."

Her eyes grew wide. "Seriously?"

"You can add some cream if you like. I like it better without."

"I thought it would be way more complicated."

"Sorry to disappoint you."

"No. I'm not disappointed. It's just. It's not much more complicated than opening a can and I'm guessing from the smell that it's a thousand times better."

I nodded. "We just need to let it simmer for a while," I said. "To really let the flavors marry." That sounded like something Julia Child would say.

But Carmel nodded earnestly, eager to learn. "I don't think my mother ever made soup in her life."

"Mine didn't either," I said.

"That's what you should do your presentation about, Daisy Jane. Your fracking soup."

"A cooking class?" I said, wryly.

"No. You could talk about different kinds of activism, about educating people."

"But that's not activism."

"Are you crazy? Of course it is."

I put the mushroom roots and onion skins in my compost bin and put the knife and cutting board in the sink while I thought about what she had said. I needed time to think about this.

She leaned against the counter. "So you will help me figure out some soups if we ever get funding to open the café?"

"Of course," I said, and then an idea occurred to me. "You'll need dishes for your café too."

"Sure. Eventually."

I sighed. "I have four sets of china," I said. "Three more than what I need."

"You could try selling it on eBay or something," she said.

"I just want to find a good home for it," I said. "That and a million other things. Want to have a look?"

She walked into my dining room where the china still sat on the table, as if displayed for a trousseau tea. There was Arthur's mother's china—plain white circles with silver bands at the edge, my mother's pink flowery fluted plates and bowls, my grandmother's yellowed china, and the pale blue-edged china my grandmother had started to buy me even before I met Arthur.

"These look like apple blossoms," Carmel said, with a wistful smile, fingering my mother's china. "But I'd have to cook fancier food to use these."

I shook my head. "You wouldn't. There's no fine china police watching to make sure you make Yorkshire pudding."

She laughed. "Well good, since I don't even know what Yorkshire pudding is."

"Would you like them? For the café?"

She smiled. "They're beautiful but they won't feed Aurora and me."

"Sure they could," I said. "I'm not asking you to buy them. I'm asking you if you'd like them as a gift."

"You're too sweet," she said, taking her hand off the plates. "I can't take something like this as a gift."

"I meant it would be your gift to me. As my sister-in-law says, 'I'm drowning in china, honey.'"

She traced her finger around the edge of a plate and smiled. "Seriously?"

"It's like that old myth about the king who didn't clean his stables out for thirty years and then needed someone to divert a river to get rid of all the mess."

I had read once about a village in England where it appeared the church had sunk into the ground until someone realized that actually the number of bodies buried in the graveyard around the church was so plentiful that the combined weight had raised the ground by a matter of inches and feet. I feared with everything I collected being inside the house and garage, that the opposite would happen, that my house would sag and sink under the weight of its collections. Because after a time, they weren't exactly mine anymore, other than to dust.

After Nick left, I found new energy in cleaning the house

out. I seconded Lee to help me carry boxes to the garage. I purged and purged. It was hard to say what it was that had made me keep everything for so long—a kind of inertia, really—and what made me finally able to see that I was never likely to have another fondue as long as I lived, that I did not need my ancient polyester maternity clothes any more.

"I had something like this," Lee said, looking over at the box of clothes I carried. "Back in the late '60s when I was pregnant."

I stopped, relieved that she was saying something to me, wondering if by showing her my collections, by the vulnerability of purging my house, I had helped her to trust me.

"The school let me take a semester off to go down to Florida with my mother so the students wouldn't see the unmarried pregnant professor."

I shifted the box on my hip. Lee held the dress against herself and then folded it up. "And then I did what all good unmarried mothers did and gave him up for adoption. And came back and taught Chaucer."

"I didn't know," I said. Technically I mostly had not.

"No one did," she said. "I think it was before you moved to Ithaca. I think about him every year on his birthday and I googled the name I gave him once, but aside from that, I barely thought about him again for most of my life. This year, I've thought about him almost constantly."

I had no idea what kinds of questions were appropriate in this situation. Could I ask her if she had regrets about her

decision or would that only wound her more? How long
had she kept him? Did she ever try to contact him? Would
she now? Had he tried to contact her? I thought of Nick and
my happy pregnancy with him, how very wanted he had
been, how much I had loved being pregnant with him, how
tenuous I had felt until I was as big as a house, how sad I had
been at never being able to be pregnant again, how much
I had loved having a baby to hold, how proud I had been
when people complimented me in the supermarket about
my beautiful baby boy. I could not imagine Lee's reality. If I,
with my son who must be only a few years younger than Lee's
child now, expressed sorrow, would that only sting?

"I don't know what to say," I said. "Thank you for telling
me."

"I called him Paul," she said. "My family never spoke of him
again after he was adopted. I wonder if we would have ruined
each other. I wonder whether I'm a grandmother somehow. I
hope his parents were good to him."

"Do you want to find him?" I asked. I couldn't help myself:
if it were my Nick, I would move heaven and earth to find
him.

"I don't know," she said. "I do, but what do I have to offer?
What do I even have to show for the choices I've made?"

I reached a hand out to her. I thought of all the times I had
felt inadequate in the conversations she and Arthur had had,
conversations peppered with words that ended in -ology.
Now that was all swept away.

"I loved my work, Daisy," she said. "But I keep thinking

about the ruins in Pompeii, and how their lives were struck down in an instant by the volcano, and that's what retirement feels like to me. I'm teaching Weng to say her L's correctly and I'm counting down the days until baseball season."

We stood in the garage and it smelled of fuel and it was cold.

"Can I help you at all?" I said because helping was what I did.

"You've saved my life," she said. "Letting me stay here. I think I would have gone insane on my own. Possibly actually insane. But I need something more and so far I have no idea what."

"That's why I'm taking the fracking course," I said. "Because I spent all last summer with Oprah Winfrey and watching celebrity gossip shows."

She raised her eyebrows.

"He died without warning," I said. "Just like Pompeii."

"But I chose this, Daisy. We don't have to retire at a certain age. We're allowed to keep going. I decided to retire because my back hurt when I had to lecture for too long and I hated those little devices, the smartphones, the students carried around. I figured I was a dinosaur and I had enough money to retire on, so I did."

"You could take a class," I said.

"It's not the same, learning and teaching."

"You could admit you made a mistake and ask for your job back."

"That's the only thing I want to do," she said. "But wouldn't they laugh?"

"Who cares if they do?" I said.

"I probably could have made it work with baby Paul. Hired a student to look after him while I taught and marked, and made it work. But I cared what they thought."

"I guess you'll have to decide whether you care what they think more than caring what you want," I said.

She looked at me. "It sounds so reasonable," she said. "Of course that's what I have to decide. But it's harder than it sounds. After this long of doing the same thing."

She was right and I knew it.

I sat in Arthur's study and wrote my presentation notes. Somehow it felt too easy, something I knew too well. I looked up at Arthur's books. Even with my years of typing for Arthur and all my reading in this area of fracking, new ideas continued to unfold and I kept coming across new and unknown layers of knowledge. I remembered being a little girl, believing one day I would know everything, I would read every book there was. I wondered where that ambition had gone, whether it had been a slow avalanche itself into the deeps where it had eventually settled into something that might only be excavated at great cost and causing collateral damage.

I opened one of Arthur's books at random, read about striation and let my eyes glaze over. Truth be told, I would never read all the books that were in my house. I thought again about the weight of the books, that they held our house down like tent pegs. But it was books that had fallen during the small earthquake. Weight could hold you down or it could crush you, if you weren't careful.

I had been crushed this morning when I had turned the calendar to December and saw the booking for the Taughannock Farms Inn, the reminder scrawled there last January as if certain.

Arthur had booked our honeymoon at the Taughannock Farms Inn, a stately mansion with private rooms and gracious staff. It reminded me of the south, even while snowflakes fell thickly outside in what was a kind of old-fashioned start to winter. We ate prime rib and Yorkshire pudding, and I learned that Arthur loved oatmeal for breakfast. We bundled up and walked along the lake shore and then up the valley to the falls, which weren't entirely frozen in December. I remember how alert I was to every little thing on our honeymoon—to the staff who, rightly but impossibly, called me Mrs. Turner, to the feeling of sleeping in a bed with someone else, to the strange weight of a gold ring on my finger. The sky was heavy but my heart was light all that week.

And maybe that's what it was that made us say a quick yes to Cornell a few years later when they offered Arthur a position in the geology department, the lovely week we had had there. We drove into town and discovered the university, which looked like castles on the hillside, especially in the snow. I had heard of Cornell University, the way you know Harvard and Yale, but I had never thought about where it was; if I had been asked, I would have said New England. I assume Arthur had known where it was, but I don't know.

Every year we went back to Taughannock Inn for our anniversary, even after we lived all of twenty minutes from it. Every time we ate the same meal and we walked down to the lake and up to the falls. We only missed the year that Nick was a baby, I think, and one year when Arthur was on sabbatical in the fall and we were in England. That meant we had spent 38 nights under its roof. And we were booked there for our fortieth.

I tried to imagine what I would do that day, what I would want to do. I could keep the booking, go and reminisce, eat what we had always eaten. I could call people up, could keep myself occupied and busy, to try to forget. I could go somewhere else, enjoy a fresh start. I had no idea what I wanted to do.

I decided to go through the shelves one by one, to look for titles that I wanted to keep, books that either reminded me of Arthur or that might be helpful in my study of fracking. The rest I would donate to the university. My neck began to ache from tilting it sideways as I moved around the room. I found seven books, one on hydrofracking that had been written in the late 1970s, two that were children's books on geology that Arthur had used to try to capture Nick's imagination, and the remainder were Arthur's three books and a book to which he had contributed a chapter.

I found a book of poetry. The book had been Arthur's, from his undergraduate days, I supposed, or even high school. I moved to the window sill and looked in the index. I found sonnets—I had not been sure exactly what sonnets were—and turned to them. I read aloud, listening for the rhythm that captivated Henry. The poetry rocked like a heart thumping. It was soothing and the rhymes were sometimes clear and sometimes almost hidden. But behind the archaic language, the rhymes, in the middle of the structure and the shape, remarkably was something vibrant and rich, filled with feeling. I had never been a dirty limerick lover like Jane, but poetry had always seemed like something sentimental. I had been surprised by Henry liking it, because nothing about Henry said sentiment to me. I put the book in my pile, intending to give it to him.

Nick had suggested I could give Arthur's books away. "You could do it gradually," he had said. "Set up a book award in Dad's name and give away a book a year." I had decided to give all the books to the university and let them choose which to keep, but I wondered as I sat in the study about setting up a scholarship in his name. Or perhaps in our names. I called the office at the university and they asked me to come in to talk about it.

"What do you want the money to do, Mrs. Turner?" the smooth man asked me the next afternoon. He had talked about annuities and perpetuity already and now he wanted me to express my own ideas.

"I'd like to set up a research grant available to anyone

researching hydraulic fracturing." Suddenly the smooth man looked perplexed. I had forgotten that the term was a technical one. "Maybe you've seen the signs around the city?" I added. "No fracking?"

He nodded but his eyes were still glazed over. Maybe he didn't get out of the city. He didn't look like he got out of the office. "I don't want to dictate the nature of the research, but it's a new field of study in geology and it affects our community so I'd like to fund research into it. I'd like to set it up so that a faculty member or grad student, or even a visiting scholar could do a term's worth of research into fracking."

We talked then about details, but it felt right. This was my choice of what I wanted to do first with Arthur's legacy and it honored his support for scholarship and new ideas. It felt like the first partnership Arthur and I had perhaps ever had— apart from Nick—a place where our interests and passions collided. I felt closer to him than I had in months.

"What do you want to call the award?" the smooth man asked eventually, as we talked about the details.

I thought for a moment. "The Arthur and Daisy Turner Hydraulic Fracturing Research Award. No." I paused and smoothed my skirt. "The Arthur and Daisy Jane Turner Hydraulic Fracturing Research Award." Yes. Yes.

Carmel had said she would call me by both names until I decided which one I wanted. I had thought long and hard about it, about reclaiming my old name, about the awkwardness of having to forever introduce myself with a

new name to people who had known me for thirty-five years.
I liked how Carmel said my names—they sang together
rather than opposing one another.

12
Carrot-Dill Soup

I had missed my October blood donation because I had been sick. When the notice arrived in the mail reminding me it was time to make another donation, I felt compelled to go right away. Donating blood had been my response to Arthur's illness; it was something I could offer. I could give life.

When I arrived at the church, a car was backing out of a parking space. I waited as the driver backed up and then, just as I was about to maneuver into position, I saw that the other driver was Cecily.

"Are you following me?" she asked with a smile. "I see you at church and at supper on Wednesday nights."

"Are you going back to work now?" I asked.

She nodded. "I'd better run. Happy donating."

I pulled into the spot and took my purse and my novel from the front seat of the car and went inside to join the assembly line. I was about to take a seat when I saw a hand waving. It was Henry. He patted the seat next to him and I went over.

"I didn't know you were a blood donor," he said.

"I'm a regular. You?"

"The same."

A nurse came into the room then and pointed at Henry

and me and another woman. I found a place for my coat and followed them into the gymnasium, which was covered in cots. The nurse directed Henry and me to cots across from one another. We both lay down on our beds and got hooked up to the machines and then they covered us with blankets.

"Come here often?" Henry said and I laughed. "I've been meaning to ask you," he said. "Your friend Carmel calls you Daisy Jane. What's with that?"

Could I bear him knowing? "My real name is Jane," I said. I watched the ground shift beneath him as if a wave had lifted him out of place and set him down in a slightly different place. I saw his eyes evaluate me differently.

"Jane. Daisy's not your real name?"

"I must have been all of four when I picked every daisy in my mother's rock garden and was found surrounded in a sea of white and yellow. My plan—I remember it—had been to make a special arrangement, with me at the center, and for my mother to find it and be delighted. Instead there were tears—both hers and mine—a spanking and then a nickname that stuck."

"Stuck?"

"I've gotten used to it after all these years. But I decided, when I took this fracking course, to use my real name again. Only I forgot and I said Daisy Jane and Ben thought I said Daisy Chain, and Carmel said she'd call me by both names until I decided which one I wanted to use."

"And have you decided?"

I nodded. "I'm using both names."

"Daisy Jane. You know we daisy-chain electrical circuits,"
Henry said. "It's not something that usually works well on a
large scale—usually people do it at home with power cords,
but it's a solution we can use to connect a variety of wires and
lines together, like a daisy chain."

I lay back and looked at the ceiling and felt the almost
imperceptible tug of the needle in my arm.

"Do you remember that wheel I brought for your son?"

I smiled. I had not thought of it for years. It had looked
like a big wooden spool and it had once contained miles of
electric wire. It had been a table and a fort and a spaceship
and still it sat in my backyard, now a planter for mint, and I
had forgotten that Henry was that same Henry. It had come
at a time when I noticed precisely no one. At least that was
how I remembered that time. The only person I noticed in
those years was Nick; I measured and planned and listened
and watched Nick with the greedy eyes of a mother with one
child, the apple of her eye. I thought everyone should adore
Nick and largely they did.

"I saw you once years ago, you and your son," Henry
said. "He was very small then. I saw you from on top of
a cherry picker. You were walking home with Nick and it
was summertime and it was hot and steamy and there had
been a sudden downburst, one of those summer storms. It
wasn't safe for me to climb down and so I was up there and I
watched you walking along, your hair plastered to your head
and your clothes stuck to your body. I had known you at the
Wednesday suppers but that day I saw everyone else scurry

for cover from the rain and you didn't. You were going to get wet anyhow so you decided to let yourself get drenched. You were carrying your shoes and walking along steaming pavement in your bare feet. And you were laughing and you had on a summer dress.

"The next Wednesday, Jane and I came to dinner like we always did, and your hair was done and you had on some other dress and you fed us all and everything. I had seen through something about you, seen past the properness, seen you. It was summertime. I think you had flowers on your dress.

"We had found out we probably couldn't have kids not long before that, and Jane was pretty fine with it but I was still broken up. I thought that's what it was. I thought it was that you were a beautiful young mother and I wished I could have that too. It wasn't something I thought about all the time, but I never forgot it either, and then when Jane got sick, everything changed and what I wanted was to run and jump in the puddles like that."

Did I even remember that day? Yes, I actually did. Did I have any idea I was being watched from above? Why no. I hadn't exactly looked up. The rain was that hard. I do remember laughing. I remember giving up and letting the rain have its way with me. I remember standing on the back porch and squeezing the rain out of my dress and my hair and letting Nick strip off and run around naked in our backyard.

I always felt spent after donating blood, not dizzy or faint, but a pleasant sense of fatigue mingled with satisfaction. They unhooked me from the machines first and I was walking toward the fellowship hall where they would have tables and chairs set up, with small plastic glasses and jugs of orange juice and plates of Christmas cookies, to bolster our sugar levels, when a nurse waved at me.

"Your husband," she said, pointing behind me. And there was Henry, holding my novel, walking toward me.

"Thank you," I said, hoping he hadn't heard her words. I had been proud that I had never cut someone's food into bite-sized chunks at a dinner party, once I became a mother, but now I wondered whether there was something about me that was so used to being a wife that I gave off that illusion.

We found seats in the crowded fellowship hall, across from one another at a tiny table. Our knees bumped as we sat and it was easy just to let them rest there. We didn't say anything. We just sat and ate cookies and let our blood course through newly emptied places within us. I looked up and Henry's eyes met mine. It made me think of his lake, still and dark, resting at the end of a long season. I look a long slow breath and let it out, and more than air seemed released.

Henry handed me my novel. "Here you go, Daisy Jane."

It was a cold and windy night and Lee asked me if I wanted a cup of evening tea. I had given my presentation that evening and now I felt exhausted and I had a scratchy throat again. I said I would welcome a hot drink. But, instead of mugs, she brought back two half-finished bottles of the sparkling cider Carmel had brought for our Thanksgiving dinner.

"These are going to go flat," she said. "Were you planning to use them for something?"

I had thought of a cider-pumpkin soup but I had that day seen a ten-pound bag of carrots sprouting new leaves and whiskers in the cold cellar and had decided to go with carrot-dill instead.

I shook my head and Lee handed me a wine glass—she had managed to thread two bottle necks between the fingers of one hand and two wine stems in the other.

"Which?" she asked.

"The dry one."

We sat quietly, looking at one another as we drank cider that was nearly but not quite flat. My presentation had gone well. I had stopped shaking the minute I stood in front of the class. They had asked me questions afterwards, questions that made me see that Carmel had been right about the personal being political. I felt relieved. I was also wondering whether I was getting sick yet again when Lee spoke.

"What if I had taken the train to Venice," she said. "Instead of Pompeii. I wonder whether I would have come back here."

It was a strange question, I thought, perilously close to regret. Asking what if was a game that could unlock decisions long made, tilt them into new combinations, like a rose window turning kaleidoscope.

"How about you?" Lee said, draining her glass. "What decisions do you ever second-guess, Daisy?"

"What if I hadn't dyed my hair," I said, weakly. This wasn't a game I was sure I wanted to play. My eyes stung and I could feel a tickle in the back of my throat.

Lee looked at me as if she were disgusted. "I mean turning points. Little decisions that end up meaning one future and not another."

"How do you know," I said. "Exactly which little decisions are the pivotal ones?"

"Because things pivot afterwards. What if I hadn't given up the baby? What if I had told the father? What if I'd listened to my parents instead of my aunt and had never pursued higher education? What if I'd never read *Wuthering Heights*? What if my father had had a son to take to baseball games instead of me? What if—you get the picture." She poured more cider into my glass. I couldn't taste the alcohol in cider, unlike wine, which was also kind of dangerous. I had forgotten it was alcoholic and had drained my glass too quickly. I thought of Carmel and the night of the Northern Lights, the what if's of that night. I got up and set up a fire in the fireplace, thinking and making sure I didn't feel lightheaded. The kindling caught easily and I watched old printouts of Arthur's shrivel under the flame, his measurements and data rise into ash and up the chimney.

What if anything, I thought, suddenly dizzy and not from alcohol. What if I'd never picked those g.d. daisies and had always been Jane? What if I'd been a debutante at the golf club as Mother had wanted? What if I'd been able to have that brood of children I had wanted? What if I hadn't seen those fracking signs? What if Arthur was still alive? What if he hadn't left me so much insurance money?

"What if I'd never suggested Wednesday suppers?" I said, returning to my chair, the fire crackling and popping behind me.

"That's a decent one," said Lee. "Think of all the people you might not know."

"What if I had gone to Europe after high school instead of getting married?"

"You got married straight out of high school?" she said.

"Nearly."

"I guess when you know, you know," she said, draining the last of the bottles into our glasses. I took a sip. The mixture wasn't bad. I felt warm from the inside and out and my throat felt marginally better. Oh, I thought, this isn't so bad.

"What if I had gotten married?" she said.

"You still could."

She threw me a look. For years I had had bad dreams about the idea of remarrying— dreams where the main feeling was one of weariness, at having to uproot everything, to begin the whole process anew. Lee had uprooted her life and had moved in with me, but I think both of us knew that it was an utterly different thing than a marriage.

"What if my son had come home for Thanksgiving?" Lee said and there was a catch in her voice. In the silence, I thought about all the choices I had made and those I had not.

And then, even as I got sicker, my choices continued to unfold. Kathy, the journalist from my class, began a series of pieces in the newspaper about fracking and the anti-fracking movement in Ithaca. She mentioned my fracking soup, Wednesday night dinners. On Wednesday, people brought copies of the article and we celebrated with glasses of cider and bowls of carrot-dill soup. I was still cautious about letting Wednesday nights be dominated by fracking; I wanted people of all types to be welcome, but that was precisely what the article had said.

I called Kathy to thank her for conveying my position so well.

"Daisy Jane," she said. "I had a call from a group of people who are forming a Listening Project. They wanted to talk with you, to ask you to be one of the listeners. Are you okay if I give them your contact info?"

My head ached and I needed to blow my nose. "Sure."

It is an intimate thing to feed someone. Even in my feverish state, I knew that. Once again I was sick. And once again Henry stood in my kitchen, but this time he was spooning honey into my throat, my mouth opening and closing. I knew we had crossed a line. I could see it on his face too.

He had believed he had come over out of kindness—dear man was characterized by kindness through and through. He had called that morning to talk to Lee, but Lee was at the university, and there was no disguising the rasp of my voice, the dulling of my sinuses. He had insisted on coming over to give me the remedy his mother had in fact given him. But this was nothing parental, nothing like mere friendship.

Sometimes, I had heard, before the advent of chloroform, women in labor were given spoons to bite on when the pain became too great. I was tempted to clamp onto the spoon with my teeth, the ache was as sudden and intense as a contraction, an ache where I had not ached in years. It felt like something utterly new, in fact. If I did bite on the spoon, he wouldn't expect that: the question was would he drop the spoon altogether or would he be drawn in, as a fish links to a fisherman?

Our eyes met for one naked moment as the spoon slid out of my mouth.

I thought of him every single time I put a spoon in my mouth, every time I felt its curve against my tongue and teeth. It made me blush to think of having soup in his presence, made me think of him over oatmeal in the morning and yogurt at night. When I licked a spoon clean of honey, I would catch my breath.

Above all else, I felt surprised—a bit bewildered as if I had awoken from a deep sleep into a very bright world where every sense was suddenly alert.

I didn't know what to do with the energy and so I walked. I walked and I walked in the early December evenings, restless and pent up. I wished I had taken on Carmel's dog after all; a dog would have given me such an excuse to walk for hours. What I wanted was at the very edge of my consciousness, but I would not look directly at it, would not let myself quite name it. I knew it as an ache. I made myself think instead about the Listening Project: they wanted people to talk with citizens, to listen to their ideas, to identify potential allies, but not to force ideas on them. I had said yes without hesitation.

As I came back to my house, I thought of a dream I had once had about a professor who came to Cornell on sabbatical. He had long hair, beautiful hair, like the mane of a horse. I remember wishing I could trade hair with him. And then I dreamed about him and it was an utterly sexual dream and I remembered precisely nothing of it when I woke up, remembered nothing in fact until I saw him on Wednesday and my face flooded with embarrassment and I remembered every single detail and I could barely face him, knowing what we had done.

It was a bit like that now with Henry. I didn't want to face him on Wednesday night. I stood on the glassed-in front porch and wondered whether I had walked enough yet to weary myself. Certainly my knees were protesting.

I shivered and realized no one had changed the screen for glass on our storm door before winter. It was cold now. The next morning, I found the pane of glass for the storm door and I sealed it tightly with a tube of caulking I bought at the hardware store. The man at the store had promised I wouldn't have any drafts, but still, as I stood looking out the glass door, I shuddered again, as if with cold.

"I'm donating most of Arthur's books to the department," I told Ben after the last class of the term.

"You're in over your head?" he said, patronizingly.

"That's not kind," I said, looking straight at him. I had decided that I was the one who had picked the daisies so I would keep that name, but I would not hide the Jane in me either. I could be both. I could be hostess and activist, I could be polite and speak up. "It's also not true." I could speak and I could be silent.

"I'm sorry, Mrs. Turner," he said. "You're right. I'm being an ass."

I let silence speak for me. And then, after a pause, I did speak. "I've enjoyed the course immensely," I said. "It's been good to stretch my brain and to learn and to figure out where I stand on the issue. I wanted to let you know I appreciated the way you made the course work for the non-geologists in the crowd, like me."

He had the grace to blush and look down. Ben always seemed to be trying to prove something, to fight a battle he didn't realize he had already won.

"I thought about keeping the books," I said. "But I realized I can always borrow them if I need them."

"Do you mind my asking what—?"

"I'm going to do some listening," I said. "Thank you, Ben. And here is my paper."

"Thank you, Daisy," he said.

"Daisy Jane," I said.

He nodded. "Daisy Jane."

13
Miso and Greens Soup

We cross lines in conversation—we ask a question that goes beyond the surface even a little and we cross a line. Or rather, more often, we don't cross those lines. We stick to the conventional and the obvious, the weather and the news. But those lines, when breached, are ones that lead us deeper, taking neighbor or classmate toward friendship. These are not fault lines.

In my conversation with Henry, we avoided crossing those lines and this made me scream inside my head, although I wore placidity like a garment. Was it true that we never really changed? Because what had been natural to me now felt like disguise, that single I could not be what I had been married, not even by half. I was wholly other than I had been, and was recovering something that had been long buried. And that was the danger in talking with Henry, because conversation with Henry unburied things, dug things up that perhaps should stay covered and safe.

Let me be blunt. There are barriers around a marriage, things that are not spoken of outside the walls of the home, things that would be a betrayal of home. There's nothing wrong with that. It's intimacy from the outside really. I had always known what my barriers were and lived comfortably within them, but now I had no idea. Henry talked to me from a need to speak or burst, that was quite clear, but his speaking nonetheless betrayed the intimacy of his marriage. And that was the thing. He had to speak of Jane in a way that took him outside the circle. And brought me into it.

But, even still, there was space for me to come and go, until one day Henry closed the gap. Until that day, I had wondered whether it was merely my imagination, my suspicion, my hunger.

Before he left my house on Wednesday night, he asked me whether I would consider meeting him at his cabin. I looked into his eyes, as deep and dark blue as the lake, and he nodded. That was all. The conversation had moved onto my front porch. I had served a miso and greens soup, warm and savory. People often mistook miso for a beef broth.

There were still people nearby and Cecily was inside and Lee. I could have believed I had misconstrued his meaning, but I did not think I had. I did not believe that he would have asked me had he not known that I knew.

So much could be contained between the lines of a sonnet, the layers of shale, the space between racks in a hive. Was the whole world ready to be sprung, ready for release? My toes curled inside my shoes but aside from that I didn't move. I might have blinked but I didn't swallow.

"I'd like that," I saw myself say, watching my breath puff out in clouds of steam in the night air.

He nodded again and said goodnight. He had told me what electrical shock felt like, the ringing in the ears, the sensitivity through the entire body, the slight weakness and the gratitude for being alive. He had said you never knew whether the gratitude was simply physical or whether it was the brush with mortality and the escape, but you noticed everything.

I looked around my house as I went inside. I heard Lee and Cecily in the kitchen. I saw the stack of books ready to go to the university, the empty floor where we had pulled up the shag carpet, Lee and I. I saw that there was new space in my life at last after years of being buried. I thought of the bee skep at the market and I thought maybe I would pick it up next week after all.

And then my legs felt weak and I sat in a chair in the living room, and Cecily came out to do one last check for bowls and saw me.

"I'm just tired," I said, but I thought then of Jane. Henry's Jane whose legs were always weak and for whom tiredness was not a lie or an excuse. Jane who could no longer manage the trip to the cabin, who was no longer a sparkplug or dazzled like fireworks. Jane who very well might have taken a lover years before if the positions were reversed.

And I had said the word to myself. Lover.

Mrs. J. Daisy Turner and her lover.

My heart settled and I went into the kitchen and talked about something or other with Lee and Cecily, and they had boiled the kettle and we had tea and then Cecily went home and Lee went to bed and I could hear her snoring from two floors away.

I wondered whether Henry snored. And whether that was part of the invitation. And how cold it might be at the cabin in December. And how this time last year I was planning for our anniversary and Christmas and sleeping down the hall from Arthur who did not snore but whose breathing reassured me, like the sound of the sea, sifting in and out. And now here I was. Had I said yes? The truth had tumbled out of me, been called out of me—that I would like to go.

My favorite crime writer said that a murder was never a moment in the making but years and years of layers until a moment came where everything tipped, like a slow underwater avalanche. It felt very inevitable tonight, very simple and easy and right. It had begun in pure kindness and grief, moments of shared consolation and laughter, passion contained. The danger of this was that this wasn't a quick seduction, a question of chemistry. At our age, we were perhaps past that. The surprising thing was how much stronger this was than that—more than any biological urge to reproduce, pheromones or sexual chemistry, this reached to the curled-up toes of the very core of me. Even if all he was asking was for me to sit alone beside him, I would still like that.

I lay awake most of the night, not wanting to sleep, wanting to ruminate on what could be, the anticipation at once delicious and terrifying.

In the morning, I paid for my night: at nearly 59, I needed my sleep, and I found myself groggy and headachey.

And so it went: on one level, I prepared to teach my Sunday

School class on the weekend, ate meals with Lee and listened to her stories of her ESL student, wondered about the money left to me, wondered what I could do with it. On another level, I continued to excavate the house. I sent out Christmas cards with just my name on them. And at the core, I thought about going to Henry's cabin. I felt more complicated than I had been in years.

I was packing but I wasn't sure what I was packing for. I had reservations at the inn that, from the room we always rented, gave a glimpse of the lake dark as ink and the trees dusty brown that ringed the lake and rose from it. Occasionally there was snow on the branches from that view. But not this year. The black ice had melted as quickly as it had come and there was still no snow. And I still didn't know whether I would keep my reservation or not. If I didn't show up, could I pull the widow card, say that I had been too embarrassed to cancel, too grief-stricken to actually show up alone? There was something to that. There was also something to the idea of going to Henry's cabin where we could sort things out perhaps in a way we couldn't in town. There was something about being surrounded by everything that was familiar that inhibited me from knowing my mind, knowing whether I was going backward or forward.

Either way, there wasn't a lot to pack. This year, I had not bought a gift for Arthur, nothing I had to smuggle into the car. I looked around my room. Nice underwear, a toothbrush, and something warm to sleep in. Clothes for hiking, a novel to read before bed or perhaps even during supper, as those articles for widows and other singles advised us we could do if we felt awkward eating alone. If I were alone.

I had not cancelled the reservation when they called to remind me about it, and I told Lee I was going out of town for the night, that it was Arthur's and my anniversary and that I needed some time to reflect. All of which was true.

I thought back to the question I had asked Lee: about whether to care more about what others thought or what you wanted yourself. No one would know if I went to the lake with him, if I lay down beside him on the camp bed, if I let him kiss me here and there. No one would know but the bees, drowsing in their hives, eating the honey they had stored away, keeping one another warm against the winter cold, taking turns fanning one another, moving to the center for warmth. There was a Bible verse about two under the same blanket on a cold night gaining warmth from each other. I remember what it said next: but how can one be warm alone? I was so tired of being alone. I could picture the wool blanket in Henry's cabin. It was green and faded. It probably smelled musty, but it was wool and wool kept body heat in beautifully. I could imagine the heat of Henry's body against mine. Oh God, I could. And I knew the brokenness of his heart and he knew mine. And from all he had said, Jane would not fault him, would have done the same thing.

A long slow avalanche was how the Marcellus Shale had

formed. The slowness of the avalanche was the thing—like a glacier advancing or retreating, such movements took such a long time that sometimes in the moment, everything probably seemed entirely still. Were there ever earthquakes, sudden quick ruptures that changed things quickly or was it all a slow dance? No one was there to watch long enough: what happened was only visible in hindsight, in the rock formation. Would fracking be as deadly as they worried it would be? Would natural channels connect and form conduits for chemicals that would destroy the groundwater? Or would they offer an innovative source of energy that would allow us to continue to drive and fly and live our suburban lives as we always had? I thought of Henry's bees and the colony collapse he feared. No one knew what the tipping point was—what would make a queen abandon her hive. Only that it happened.

And yet, this was all too metaphorical for what was. A beautiful man wanted me to go out of town with him. Perhaps to commit adultery. My husband was dead and I was free to move on; only Henry and Jane knew what was between them, and Henry felt free to ask me to join him. If Jane had also died, would I have gone there? Yes.

I thought of Henry's body, honed by climbing power lines and by running along country roads, lifting supers of honey and helping Jane in her everyday tasks.

I needed to go see Jane. I had never been to their house before and I looked them up in the phonebook and found their address. I ladled leftover miso soup into a yogurt container and wedged it onto the seat beside me in the car. I drove up their street and there was no car in the driveway, but I couldn't park there. I drove around the block and parked the car near the lake. The sky was heavy and low, and my knees ached from the damp cold. I wondered whether Henry had gone to the cabin at the small lake, whether that lake was frozen over. Here the lake had a thin layer of ice on the surface in the bay at our end of the lake, but I could see open water to the north. There was a story that circulated at the college that if the lake froze over completely, classes would be cancelled for the day. There had been a day when that happened, but only once in living memory.

I walked up the steps to Jane's house and knocked on the door. No one answered. I knocked again. Maybe they were out at a doctor's appointment, I thought, or visiting someone. It felt like Henry's world suddenly acquired a third dimension, that I had been looking at it from high above, from a power pole, for instance, and everything had seemed clear in its outlines, but now I had come back down to earth and could actually see the contours and relief better, could see that things were not as simple as they had appeared from high above. They had a life together, just as Arthur and I had had, filled with artifacts that told a story, told a million stories. I was trying to decide whether to leave the soup or whether it had just been an excuse when the door opened and a thin face peered out, at my waist level.

"Jane?" I said. "It's Daisy. I should have been by to see you ages ago, but I thought of you today." Yes, Mrs. J. Daisy

Turner, widow and hostess, fracktivist and student, thought
of you when your husband invited me to his cabin. "And I
thought I would bring you some soup."

She invited me in although, in her wheelchair, she couldn't
hold the door open and I had to take the soup into the
kitchen myself, while she waited in the living room, wings
clipped by multiple sclerosis. Her hair was gray now and it
stood up at the back.

"Henry's up at the lake today," she said and I couldn't meet
her eyes.

"Can I get you anything?" I asked.

"I left my drinking bottle in the bedroom," she said. "When
I came to answer the door. It would be kind if you would get
it. It's just down the hall, last door on the right."

As I walked down the hall, I thought about the Jane I had
known. Arthur had said she was snappy—she always wore
red lipstick and bright clothes and she was a career gal, as
we used to say. She had never had children and she had been
snappy about that too. Now she reminded me of a cookie that
had lost its crunch, softened with the damp.

Of course that was what was so hard on Henry, I thought.
If she weren't like this, he wouldn't be like he was either. I
opened the door to her bedroom and there was the slightest
smell of urine. The bed was unmade—had I woken her
up?—but the room was clean otherwise. I could tell which
was Jane's side of the bed—did they still share a bed, I
wondered?—because of the collection of pill bottles. I found
a drinking bottle with a Niagara Falls logo on it and carried it

out to her.

"I should have come to visit you long ago," I said. "And thank you for sending me the flowers."

She looked confused. Oh God, had he lied? "The roses from your garden?" I said.

"Oh yes. Yes. I had Henry bring them to your dinner so everyone could enjoy them. I can't smell anything anymore," she said. "Damn disease." There it was—a flash of the snappiness. It was like seeing the resemblance of a parent in a child, only in reverse—here it was the shadow of who she had been.

"That must be hard," I said. I saw that her left hand was trembling and I wondered whether that was the disease or whether she was afraid of me. I felt strangely powerful for practically the first time in my life.

"I'm sorry about Arthur," she said. "I read about it in the paper."

Now I felt myself tremble. "Thank you," I said. "It was a complete shock."

"He used to say you were his rock, Arthur did," she said, eyes drifting.

"He did?"

"It was a pun, but he meant it. He said once he hoped he died before you because he wouldn't know how to cope without you."

I looked at her watery eyes and thought she was beyond the ability to scheme or lie to make anyone feel better—or worse.

"Thank you," I said. "I never heard him say that."

"He got his wish too," she said.

She seemed glad for the company but she tired quickly and nodded off while we were talking. I cleared my throat and she woke up.

"Sorry," she said.

"I've stayed too long," I said. "Can I help you at all?"

"I'm fine," she said. "Relatively speaking."

"Of course," I said.

"Come again," she said. "Anytime. We'd love to see you."

We. She was part of a dynamic that could say we—and I was not. I found my coat in the closet and there was a scarf on the hanger I had used, Henry's scarf, and it left the scent of him on the collar of my coat.

"Take good care," I said.

"You too."

And my legs trembled as I walked down her steps, as if her disease were contagious. I made it to my car before I burst into tears.

I sat in the car and bawled, oblivious to the world around me, wiping my nose on my coat sleeve, sobbing at the top of my lungs, without thought, without words. My car steamed up so that no one could really see me, and I was glad for the privacy once I surfaced a little bit from my grief. I understood then about people who rent their garments and who poured ashes on their heads. The grief of tunafish sandwiches and Oprah in the afternoon was wholly inadequate for the well of emotion that was underneath. It could not be fracked, not safely. There was nothing safe about it. It was a tsunami, an earthquake, a tidal wave. It could drown you, throw you, destroy you, eat you alive and yet—and this was the horrible heart of grief—you stayed alive in some horrendous way, something pecking out your liver, only to have it grow again to be pecked out some more.

And then I could not sit still a moment longer. I wasn't about to walk Henry's neighborhood looking no better than I would if I had actually poured ashes on my head. I had to drive. I found a Kleenex I should have used on my nose and used it to wipe down the windows, and then I drove and drove. And as I drove, I found myself muttering and cursing every few minutes. And then continually and I had to park the car on the shoulder of the road again. When I had no words to say, when I could not tell whether my grief was for Arthur, my mother, Henry, Lee, the ache of the world, Jane, the land and the water, the sky and the sea, my son so far away on the other side of the world, or just for myself, when it all came together in a ball of pain, I moaned as I had in childbirth. They had shushed me then, they had offered me drugs to make me sleep or dope me up, and I had said no then, fierce as an animal in my pain and I said no now, and I moaned as any animal would, wounded and sore, infected with grief and aching in pain. My anger was a bright force and if I had felt powerful with Jane, I felt so much more so now. There was no hostess in me, nothing remotely civilized in the least. I ached to be touched, to be held, to be loved. I ached for it like thirst on a hot day.

And yet, in all my pain, there she sat, small and vacant and vulnerable, looking out and watching the lake freeze over and never a day off for her.

Just when I was starting to calm down, just when I had caught my breath and was either going to fall asleep as I had in labor or was going to start my car again, I thought of what Jane had said Arthur had said. Arthur who knew rocks, who loved rocks. Arthur who had not one line of poetry in him, not one metaphor to be spared. Arthur had called me his rock.

And something split inside me as it had at the moment Nick was born. At that moment, the moment he crowned and emerged into the world, what I remember was a sense of shock, of being ripped astern bodily, torn in the deepest place, splayed, rendered irreparably apart, destroyed, rescued, transformed.

And that was the moment the pain stopped. I had wondered if I was dead then and I wondered it now too. It was as if I had touched an electrical wire and been thrown far out beyond where I had ever been before. I felt stunned, silent, cold, exhausted, emptied, still.

I knew where I was going. I didn't have another Kleenex to wipe the window, so I did the best I could with the one I had, and then I opened the windows of the car and I drove until I figured out where I was and turned myself in the direction of his cabin. I drove up and down hills that were bare of leaves but that had their own kind of stark beauty, reaching naked branches toward the sky, no pretense, no covering.

A ridge of pale afternoon sunlight, the color of hope, after a day of fuzzy indistinctness, brought into relief the contours of the mountains, their particular shapes, but more than that, the heaviness of the clouds had lifted, not much—there were still dark clouds, but they were lighter and at the same time darker. Everything was not a heavy white mist that sank into the bones anymore. It was not clear weather here, not yet. But it was clear somewhere not far, near enough that the eye was drawn to the edge of the light where the land and sky met.

I drove up impossibly steep hills, past hibernating ridges and hills, fuzzy with branches, draped with fog. I had passed houses that made me itch to clean them up or out, houses that had probably gone into foreclosure, houses whose owners would see fracking as salvation. There were many ways to live, I concluded, as I drove past pre-fabricated houses, beautifully maintained wooden farmhouses and hillbilly shacks, in quick succession.

I found myself on a rutted dirt road, passing bales of hay that had been left in the field for the winter. It had been summer the last time I was at Henry's cabin. I had dangled my feet in that lake, I thought with a shiver, looking at the rim of ice that ringed the lake. The water in the center was as still as a mirror. I could hear late migrating geese complaining from somewhere on the lake.

I pulled my car behind his and wiped my eyes as clean as I could. I took a deep breath and stepped out of the car. My legs were still weak but I could stand and I could put one foot in front of the other.

He heard my car and came out of the cabin and stood in

the doorway as I approached.

"You came," he said. "I hoped you would."

"Can I come in?" I asked.

"Of course." He held the door and I could smell the same smell that was on the scarf, the same smell I had smelled in this very place in the summertime. It was the smell of a man who climbed high above the earth and handled the power of electricity in his bare hands. I do not know the geography of your body, I thought, nor do you know mine. I thought of the body I knew well, the freckles and moles, the hair sprouting, the sounds and sighs. I thought of the scars I bore, the silver lines that echoed the earthquake of my pregnancy, like aftershock or ripples. The faded scar across my pelvis: appendix.

What is there to say, to want?

It was, as I knew, a rustic place. There was nowhere to sit but on the bed. He had brought a portable heater since I had been there last. It was warmer than I had expected and I took my coat off and sat on the bed.

The light was already fading in the sky, the days were that short. It had been a day of heavy skies, but as I had walked up to the cottage, the sun had broken through the clouds over the lake, just a few rays. One of them penetrated the cabin now, through the holes between the slats of wood. It made a thin line of gold across my lap on the far side of the cabin and I touched it, breaking the line with my own shadow.

Henry stood leaning against the sink. He looked tentatively happy and beautiful and tired.

"They used to think that bees were chaste," Henry said. "Which was why nuns and monks were the beekeepers. They felt like bees were a symbol of industry and chastity. And they thought new bees spontaneously generated. You know the idea of a unicorn only being able to lay its head in the lap of a virgin? It was kind of like that. They said bees could tell a lecherous person and they would swarm and sting him. No one who ever watched a hive saw the bees mating so they thought they were celibate forever. It was only a hundred years ago that they figured out that the king was actually a queen bee and actually saw the queen and all the males mating."

I almost had to speak of Arthur, had to get his ghost out of the room, but some truths were betrayals to speak.

The line of light had moved in that short period of time, but neither Henry nor I did. I opened my hands toward the light as if it were a bar I might grip to steady myself.

"After Arthur died, I watched celebrity gossip shows on television just to keep myself from thinking, from feeling. The people on those shows, those entertainers, they call them beautiful people because they are. They're achingly lovely. Like you."

I looked up at him and I could see the line of light around his waist, like a belt wide open.

"But there's something they don't know on those shows, and that is about the beauty of keeping your word, keeping your promises, keeping yourself."

I could not look at him. I looked at the floor.

"I don't want to sit around and wonder what would have happened if I hadn't married Arthur, what would happen if Jane died. I might never have gotten to this point without the choices I made. How could those questions be useful? How could I tease out what we would have done differently, if we had the choice? That way of thinking is like the processed water that's left behind after fracking, the kind that taints the groundwater and the apples and everything that's good."

I heard a noise and I looked up. He had turned to face the wall, his hands gripping the counter, defeated. Desire for him had gripped me, had eaten me away from beneath.

"I had a poem for you," he said and his voice was broken.

"Go ahead," I said, although whether this was wise or not, I did not know.

"And, thou away, the very birds are mute/Or, if they sing, 'tis with so dull a cheer/ That leaves look pale, dreading the winter's near."

"Shakespeare?" I asked finally when he had been silent too long.

"I have no goddamn idea," he said, laughing with a choke in his voice. "Ask Lee. It's the sonnet I think of when I think of you."

He turned and sat on the counter, facing me. The light had sunk beneath the level of the counter and all the gold was gone. "But you came," he said.

I nodded and the calm that had come over me earlier was starting to ebb with the light. I thought I might cry again, thought it might be best if I didn't. And then there were tears on my cheeks.

He came over to me and put his arms around me and let me cry and lean into him for a while. It was so easy to be with him. I thought of Jane again and tried to use her tired image as a talisman against the warmth of him. I thought of Arthur calling me his rock and tried to be rocklike when everything inside me was soft and open.

No rock was stable. Everything was always in flux, even if it was a long, slow avalanche. Even a rock could be worn down by water. Henry's finger found the line of my jaw and he traced it lightly so that I stirred.

"You're beautiful," he said. I knew he hoped I could be wooed, and I knew he meant it.

"What if they discover a cure for MS tomorrow?" I said, pulling away from him and looking out the window. "Or what if she goes into remission, or what if your bee colonies don't collapse or what if she dies tomorrow? What if you make all the difference in something important?"

"People with MS normally have a regular lifespan," he said, dully. "Do you not have a morsel of pity in you?"

"Trust me," I said. "Pity is highly overrated. And no, after being faithful to my husband for 39 years, I am not about to sleep with you out of pity."

"If you think it's just that, you're wrong."

"No. I know. I know it's not."

I thought about the moment in the car when I had been cracked open, the moment the tears had stopped. I looked out the window and up in the sky and for a moment, north of the lake, I thought I saw a shimmering of light and I wondered about Carmel and her Northern Lights. And then I realized it was my city, my home, the lights of Ithaca reflected in the clouds over the horizon.

I turned back to him. Our conversation had been more intimate today than any I had ever had with a man. Perhaps that alone was a kind of unfaithfulness.

"I'm sorry, Daisy," he said again and I couldn't see his face in the shadows.

"Daisy Jane," I said inside my head, but I wasn't about to correct him just now. "You are a good man, Henry," I said aloud. "I think you need a holiday."

"I need you."

"I've been asking myself whether it was wrong to do what I wanted and then this afternoon I realized what I wanted most was not to be with you, but to be true to myself."

"But you were at least tempted?"

"I was at least tempted," I said, biting my lip.

"Will you wait for me?" he asked.

I shook my head. "Don't wait for her to die, Henry."

I walked back to my car in the dark, leaving Henry alone in the cabin. I hoped he would go home to Jane, that he would heat up the soup I had left behind.

People said grief took a year, that it took a year of occasions without the deceased, that it had to come full circle before you could fully let go. They also said that grief was an utterly unique experience for every single person, and so there was no one way to do it. What does it take to get over grief? It takes time, they say, but then I thought of Queen Victoria and her mourning that lasted far longer than her marriage ever had.

Time was not all. The other thing people suggested was starting something new. And not just anything. You could take up a hobby and be bored with the ennui of grief, the heaviness of doing something you were supposed to be enjoying. You could volunteer, get a pet, try a sport, visit a country. For Lee, it had been Pompeii and baseball; for me, it had been fracking. Something that caused a spark of curiosity, something that called out to something deep inside you. It was like any relationship: who can say why one relationship works and another does not? Or why one plant will flourish and another will wilt? I did not know what it would be for Henry. Maybe running or bees. And maybe if grief lasted long enough, it needed to be a succession of things. Like hunger, grief would return. The amazing thing was that it ever abated, that healing ever came at all.

It had been spring when my husband died, leaves newly budded and now every leaf was decaying on the ground. Death had come in the middle of life, and now, oddly enough, in the cold dark of the year, I felt new life within me.

I felt a bit callous to feel this way and leave Henry so heavy but he was not ultimately mine to worry about. Nor was Arthur. I believed Arthur had been faithful to me, but at the moment of decision, it had not been his faithfulness that had mattered, but my own. Because ultimately that was all I was responsible for, and all I could do was to walk up a path in the darkness toward the light in the distance, hoping and heading toward home.

Epilogue
Pepper Pot Soup

If Christmas fell on a Wednesday, we would cancel our Wednesday night supper but otherwise we were almost always in town and so I would make soup that week as I did every week. The crowd of people who came out the week of Christmas was always smaller, and it felt intimate being together. If the group was small enough we would gather around the dining room table, a party of exiles making a home together.

This year, Wednesday was the 23rd. I made a pepper pot soup, hot and spicy, red and green. I put the tablecloth I had picked up at the bazaar on the table, dark rich plaids. I put the Advent wreath in the center of the table and lit all the candles but the middle one.

I had made sure Carmel would be there. I had a present for her: an envelope with a check in it that would be an investment in her café. I couldn't wait to see her face. I had wrapped a box of Nick's wooden blocks for Aurora. I hoped she would be there too.

I had an announcement to make, too. Lee had agreed to make soup throughout the month of January while I traveled to Singapore to visit Nick. Cecily would help her. It was only eleven days until my plane left. When I came back, I would start my Listening Project training and I would start helping Carmel develop recipes for the café.

I also had a present for Henry: I had wrapped up Arthur's book of sonnets. He had missed last week's supper and I wondered whether he would be back.

And then, there he was, north to my compass. "Merry Christmas, Daisy Jane," he said and he handed me an enormous jar of honey.

I opened the jar and took a long sniff. "Sunshine and rain and clover and wildflowers," I said and my eyes met his, a long slow underwater avalanche.

Acknowledgements

I am not really a dog person but this book would likely not exist if it weren't for my black Lab-springer spaniel, Lucky. The year he arrived in our lives, we couldn't go to our usual beloved summer cottage because of him and so we asked around for alternative ideas. Andrea Mickie told me she had gone to Ithaca with her puppy years before, that it was dog-friendly. And so it was. We loved it. Like Daisy, I noticed roadside signs saying No Fracking—but it was months later when I thought to look the word up and then found the movie *Gasland*.

This story also sprang from another dog-related source: as I walked my puppy through our neighborhood on early-dark fall evenings, we could easily see into brightly lit windows and I began to see the beauty and the weight of collections, and the imperfect artifacts that tell the story of a life.

I want to thank many people for their support and help in writing this book. First, always, to Dave with whom I gladly share this long, slow avalanche of a life. Please don't drop dead in a faculty meeting any time soon. Then to my beloved Hopeful Writers Group—Erin Bow, Nan Forler, Kristen Mathies, Pamela Mulloy and the late Esther Regehr—who are my clan. Big thanks to my children—Matthew, John and Megan—for going with me to Ithaca again and again: as Daisy says of Nick, they are my most precious legacy. I'm conscious, too, that they are the recipients of our environmental choices.

Many thanks to early readers Bonnie Filipchuk, Penny Stevens, Rebecca Sutherns, Joanne Paterson, Lorilee Jespersen, Kristen Ciccarelli, Carol Meredith, Donna Mann, Sheri Gingerich, Cory Boyd, Susan Scott and the Somerset Avenue Book Club.

Andy Meisenheimer is a fantastic editor who nudges and pushes, slashes and suggests. Scott McIntyre brought this book to life with his design, typesetting and kindness. Patricia Bow thoughtfully and surgically proofread the book. Many thanks to Nick Lee who made the cover beautiful.

Thank you to Helen Kroeker and the staff at Elevation and St. John's who were willing to test Daisy's soups and to encourage me along the way.

Thank you to Chuck Erion and Don Pape for wise counsel and perennial encouragement. Beth Jusino, Martin Crosbie, Ray Charbonneau and Christian Snyder shared wisdom on publishing. Thanks too to the Storywell writers whose persistence, bravery and imagination inspire me, and to the Monday Morning Group at Death Valley's Little Brother.

My parents—Bob and Carol Meredith—and my inlaws— Don and Marjorie Fish: thank you for your encouragement and love.

I think of women I know who have walked some of this valley, and from whom I borrowed the barest bones. I appreciate conversations with Jacob Pries about how someone becomes an activist. Thank you to Dr. Theo Colborn, Wilma Subra, Rachel Carson and Elizabeth May for pioneering the way.

I am grateful for the City of Ithaca, NY, and all my happy places there: the market, Wegmans, the top of Robert H Treman Park (although I haven't been able to bring myself to climb down Lucifer Falls), the Moosewood, Maté Factor Café, Bluebird Antiques (where I found Daisy's apron), the Lions Club Community BBQ at Cass Park, and the Cayuga Lake Creamery. Thank you to Elan and Rachael Shapiro of the Frog's Way in the Eco-Village.

Thank you to The Civil Wars whose song *The Violet Hour* formed the (short) soundtrack to this book. Thanks to Crieff Hills, where I write and see most clearly.

Susan Fish
October 2014

About the Author

Susan Fish lives in Waterloo, Ontario, Canada. Her first book *Seeker of Stars* was published in 2005 and reissued in 2013.

susanfishwrites.wordpress.com